The

and

The Cowboy.

by

MAGGIE CARPENTER

 This book is a work of fiction. The characters, incidents, and dialogue are drawn from the author's imagination and are not to be construed as real. Any resemblance to actual events or persons, living or dead is entirely coincidental.

Cover Design
Fantasia Frog Designs
https://fantasiafrogdesigns.wordpress.com/
Published by: Dark Secrets Press

Visit Maggie Carpenter
http://www.MaggieCarpenter.com
https://www.facebook.com/MaggieCarpenterWriter

CHAPTER ONE

Sitting back in the Adirondack chair on the porch of his luxury mountain cabin, Clint Kincaid glanced up at the sun slowly disappearing behind the towering pine trees and let out a contented sigh. He'd arrived a week before, and though winter was waning and spring was in the air, there was still a smattering of snow on the ground. He savored the change of seasons, and the cold, overnight temperatures.

Clint owned a chain of western wear, tack and feed stores, and for years he was only able to use the remote hideaway for short breaks or executive retreats. But the long hours and hard work had paid off. Now he lived there in the spring, summer and early fall. In the winter months the harsh conditions made it impossible.

Earlier in the day, he had taken Leroy, his brown and white paint, and Buck, his big, long-haired, mixed breed dog, on an extended trail ride. There was nothing they liked better than to head out on long treks. Now Buck was feverishly devouring a rawhide next to him, and Leroy was happily munching his well deserved hay in the small barn.

With the sun quickly sinking, Clint rose from his chair and ambled away from the cabin. It was time to settle his beloved horse in for the night.

"Well, Leroy, you get a good night's sleep," he muttered, walking into the stable and throwing a warm blanket over the gelding's back, but as he fastened the straps he heard Buck barking.

The dog didn't react to the wildlife.

Hastily grabbing the rifle from its rack on the wall, Clint peered out the window. Not seeing anything, he moved cautiously through the door—then stopped short, scarcely believing his eyes. A dark-haired young woman was sliding off a big-boned, dapple grey mare.

"Thank God," she moaned, staring across at him. "If I hadn't found you…"

"What the hell…?" he exclaimed. "Who are you, and what the blazes are you doin' up here?"

She started to reply, but suddenly tumbled to the ground.

Quickly resting his rifle against the barn wall, he moved swiftly towards her with Buck running excitedly alongside. But as he neared, he slowed his step and ordered his dog to stop so he wouldn't spook the horse.

"Easy," he said softly, sliding the reins over its head, then scooped the girl into his arms. With Buck racing ahead, Clint hastily returned to the barn, evoking a loud whinny from Leroy as he entered.

"What's happening?" the girl asked breathlessly, slowly opening her eyes.

"You passed out," Clint replied, sitting her on a bale of hay. "Wait here while I take care of your horse," then noticing how cold she was, he removed his jacket and placed it around her shoulders.

"Molly, her name is M-Molly," the girl muttered.

As he removed the mare's saddle he could see she was well muscled. But it made sense. She couldn't have made it up the long trail if she hadn't been. Leading her into a stall, he slid off the bridle, then threw on one of Leroy's blankets, filled the water buckets and dropped a flake of hay into the feeder.

"I'll take you into the cabin, then come back and check on her in a little while," Clint declared, walking back to the girl still shivering beneath his jacket.

"My hands are s-so c-cold," she whimpered as he helped her stand up. "I forgot to bring gloves."

"You came into the mountains without gloves?"

"I, uh, I was in a hurry."

"Apparently," he remarked as he guided her from the barn and across to the cabin with Buck beside them. "I'll make you some hot chocolate, but you have to tell me what you're doin' up here and how you found me. I'm Clint Kincaid, by the way."

"I'm Tiffany Sullivan."

"That's Buck," he continued as he opened the front door and the dog raced past them. "He's a big boy and has a lot to say for himself, but he's harmless."

Not sure if he should continue to quiz her or wait until the morning, he settled her into the chair closest to the fire and moved into the kitchen. But as he set about making the hot chocolate, his concern for her became tinged with anger.

"Uh...do you know Devlin Pike?" she asked as he carried the steaming mug into the living room. "He owns a cabin somewhere in this area."

"Sure, it's not as far up and further east."

"That's where I was headed," she said as she accepted the welcome drink. "I must have made a wrong turn. Molly and I do endurance riding, but even for us it had been a tough trip. Anyway, I suddenly had no idea where I was, then I saw the smoke from your chimney. I thought about going back and trying to find the right trail, but we were both so tired and the sun was setting."

"But why did you head up the mountain with no supplies and by yourself? Was Devlin expectin' you? If he was he'll be worried. We need to call him."

"Uh, no, he's not there. This hot chocolate is so good."

"You haven't answered my question," he said sternly. "Why were you making such an arduous ride unprepared? Are you runnin' from the law?"

"Of course not," she shot back. "Sorry," she added quickly. "It's just..."

"Just what? You should have your ass spanked for makin' such a dangerous journey."

A pink tinge crossed her cheeks, and he wondered if it was from his sharp rebuke, or if his wild guess had been right. She was in trouble even though she'd denied it. He needed answers, and he didn't want to wait.

"Out with it, Tiffany. Why did you come up here alone and unprepared?"

CHAPTER TWO

Arriving at Clint's cabin had been no accident, and Tiffany had known exactly who the handsome cowboy was when she'd seen him.

But everyone in the western world knew Clint Kincaid.

He was legendary.

He'd started selling used tack and western show clothes at flea markets when he was still in high school, and opened his first storefront at only twenty-one.

But still in two minds about telling him why she was there, and afraid he would see right through her, she quickly lowered her eyes.

"I'm waitin'," he said, his voice still stern.

Slowly lifting her gaze, she risked catching his eye. He appeared to be either annoyed or worried, perhaps both. Regardless, she had to say something.

"Are you in trouble with the police?" he asked just as she was about to speak. "Is that why you were hightailin' it to Devlin's cabin? Were you plannin' on hidin' out until you could decide what to do?"

She caught her breath. Devlin's cabin had never been her destination. She'd been heading to Clint's home from the start. But she'd underestimated how long it would take and how arduous the journey would be. Her exhaustion was all too real.

"No and yes," she finally managed. "I'm not in trouble with the sheriff, and I understand why you need to know how I came to be here. But I need to catch my breath. I don't feel very well. In fact, I'm starting to feel cold again, and dizzy."

What she'd said had been the truth, but as his eyes narrowed, it was apparent he was doubting every word.

"It'll be dark soon. You won't be goin' anywhere so I guess it can wait a bit. I'll show you to the guest room. You should get some proper rest and I've got some things to do. I'll be makin' supper around seven—unless you're hungry now."

"No, I feel sort of sick. Rest sounds wonderful though," she added, relieved she'd bought herself some time. "I ache everywhere."

"After that ride I'm not surprised," he remarked, rising to his feet. "Come with me."

As she followed him across the living room and down a wide hallway, she found the cabin much larger than it appeared from the outside.

She reminded herself the man was a millionaire. He wouldn't have built himself a shack.

They passed a couple of doors, then he opened one on his left and gestured for her to enter. But stepping past him, she stopped and stared. Floor to ceiling sliders leading out to a terrace offered a breathtaking view of the rugged terrain beyond.

"It's just gorgeous," she said softly, turning to face him. "Can I ask a stupid question?"

"The only stupid questions are those that aren't asked," he replied, then smiled for the first time.

It was an engaging, seductive smile, a smile that suggested wicked secrets. Butterflies suddenly fluttered in her stomach.

"So…what is it you want to know?" he pressed, breaking into her thoughts.

"Don't you have to worry about sliding glass doors with the conditions up here?"

"No, they're tempered glass. All they require is some minor maintenance. Make yourself comfortable. I'll knock on your door when it's dinner time. If you don't answer I'll assume you're asleep and I won't bother you until morning. But, Tiffany," he added, lowering his voice, "you need to tell me what's goin' on."

Before she could respond, he quickly stepped back into the hall and closed the door behind him.

Dropping onto the bed, she began to second-guess her decision. Showing up at his home pretending to be lost had seemed like a good idea. And it had worked. She was under his roof. She would tell him about the danger she was in over dinner. But should she come clean about everything?

Suddenly caught up by a heavy yawn, she realized how desperately she needed to close her eyes.

Peeling off her clothes and letting them lie in a heap on the floor, she crawled under the covers. The bed was divine, and the sheets the softest she'd ever felt against her skin.

But most importantly, she was safe.

No-one knew where she was.

That alone would allow her to sleep for the first time in two days.

* * *

Clint had returned to the barn to check on the horses. Molly was down and sleeping, but Leroy was watching her through the wide, wooden planks.

"Keepin' an eye on her, big fella?" Clint asked softly. "I reckon we're in the same boat. But I never forget a face, and I know that girl. Still, I could've just spoken to her in one of my stores. Sure wish I could remember though."

Out of the blue, it hit him.

All he had to do was look up her name in the data base for the Elk Valley location. If she'd bought something there'd be a record of the transaction and it might jog his memory. But as he left the barn, he found himself wondering if her appearance at his cabin had been accidental...

CHAPTER THREE

As she slowly stirred from sleep, Tiffany found herself staring at bright red digits. Squinting, she read 10:04 PM. Stretching her arms above her head and looking around, she discovered the room was softly lit from a small lamp sitting on a chest of drawers against the wall. She also noticed a white bathrobe lying across the end of the bed. Though she wasn't sure if it had been there when she'd crawled between the sheets she didn't care. She was just grateful to have it.

Slipping from the bed, she wrapped it around her body and padded across to a door she assumed was the bathroom. Walking in she saw a deep whirlpool tub and stall shower, then opening the drawer under the sink, she found shower caps, sample packets of shampoo, conditioner, bath gel and a blow dryer.

"This is like a five-star hotel," she mumbled, removing a shower cap from its plastic wrap.

Covering her hair and taking off the robe, she stepped into the stall and let the hot water stream across her body. Never had a shower felt so good. Finally turning off the faucets, she quickly dried herself off with a thick, thirsty towel, put the robe back on and returned to the bedroom.

But her feet were bare, and her dirty socks lying on the floor held no appeal. Wondering if she'd find a pair in the dresser, she checked the top drawer. Brand new, thick fuzzy socks stared up at her, and she quickly discovered more clothing in the drawers below.

It occurred to her Clint probably had business retreats at the cabin, and it made sense he'd cater to his guests. Slipping on a pair of the warm, thick socks, she left the bedroom and headed off in search of something to eat.

The house was quiet, but in the lounge a couple of lamps still burned, and moving into the kitchen, she broke into a smile. A note was balanced against a small bowl with a lid, next to which were utensils wrapped in cloth napkin.

Chicken Stew. Microwave on high five minutes. Stir, then another two minutes. Help yourself to whatever else you want. There's a drinks cabinet in the living room next to the bookshelf.

Clint.

Immensely grateful, she followed the instructions, then found French rolls in the bread bin and spreadable butter in the refrigerator. Settling down at the kitchen table, she devoured the delicious meal, and had just taken her last bite when the handsome cowboy sauntered in. The timing was so perfect she wondered if he'd been watching.

"Feelin' better?" he asked, sitting opposite her.

"Almost human again," she replied, thinking he looked ridiculously handsome.

Every photograph she'd ever seen of him, he'd been wearing a hat, just as he had when she'd arrived. Now without it, she was looking at a sexy mop of unruly chestnut hair. He'd also changed out of his jeans and grey sweatshirt into khaki slacks and a forest green sweater.

"What?" he asked, looking back at her.

"You look—different," she replied, hating the warmth she could feel coloring her face. "You're not wearing a hat."

He laughed out loud.

"No, I'm not in the habit of wearin' my hat when I'm loungin' around my house at night."

"I hope you don't mind, but I nabbed a pair of socks," she said quickly, wanting to change the subject.

"That's what they're there for, to be nabbed," he remarked with a grin. "But now you're rested and fed--"

"You want some answers," she interjected.

"I was goin' to say, how about we sit in the livin' room and have a drink? But yeah. Some answers would be good."

"Sure, I'll just wash up this bowl. It was delicious, thank you."

"The bowl can wait," he said sharply as he pushed back from the table.

Taking her hand, he led her from the kitchen into the lounge and sat her on the couch in front of the fireplace.

"What'll it be?" he asked, stepping away and opening a cabinet next to the bookshelf. "I have a smooth Cognac you might like."

"That sounds great, thanks."

But watching him pour the drink into brandy snifters, she started to feel nervous. Telling her story wouldn't be the easiest thing in the world.

"There you go," he said, handing her the drink and sitting next to her.

As she took a sip, she closed her eyes and let the warm liquor slide across her tongue and down her throat.

"Wow, that is sublime. I've never tasted anything like it."

"I thought you'd enjoy it. Now, why are you here?"

"Jeez, talk about—"

"Spit it out," he said sternly.

"Do you have to be so demanding?"

"I don't like people beatin' around the bush!"

"And I don't like being interrogated!"

"Okay, let's play that old game, Truth or Dare. It helps gettin' to the nitty gritty of things."

Even though his voice had softened, her heart skipped.

"Uh, I'm not sure."

"Tiffany, I'm a patient man, but—"

"Okay, yes, maybe it will help," she said hastily, not wanting to anger him.

"Good, so, Tiffany, truth or dare?"

"Dare," she muttered, thinking it would be the safer choice to start. But as he grinned and placed his drink on the end table, she wondered if she'd just made a mistake.

"I dare you to let me hug you real tight."

It was the last thing she expected, but staring at the gorgeous man beside her, she could think of nothing she wanted more.

"Actually," she began, trying not to show too much enthusiasm as she placed her snifter on the coffee table, "I'd like that very much."

"Yeah, I thought you might," he muttered, wrapping his arms around her and pulling her into his chest. "Whatever sent you up the mountain can't get to you here. Take a breath. You're safe now."

CHAPTER FOUR

While Tiffany had been resting, Clint had found a record of her purchases, but none of them triggered any memories, and he still didn't know why she looked familiar. Though he could have simply seen her in one of this stores, he had an inkling it had been somewhere else.

Now cradling her in his arms, he could feel her melting against him. Hoping her guard would be lowered he pulled back —but as their eyes met, he suddenly felt his anger fading, and a strong desire to press his lips against hers.

"Your turn," he said softly.

"Truth or dare?" she murmured, holding his gaze.

"Truth."

She paused.

"Do you want to kiss me?" she asked as if reading his mind.

"Yes, but this isn't the time," he said, lowering his voice. "My turn. Truth or Dare?"

"Uh…I think I'll go with truth."

"Have we met?"

"Briefly, I came third in the Western Pleasure year-end championships at the county show last year, and you presented the prizes."

"That's it! I knew our paths had crossed! You were wearin' a turquoise shirt," he replied, instantly recalling how he'd thought her blue eyes sparkled like the rhinestones on the collar.

"You really do remember."

"Why didn't you mention it?" he asked, releasing her and leaning back against the couch.

"You're Clint Kincaid! I felt a bit weird."

"I wish you had. I've been rackin' my brains tryin' to figure out why I thought I knew you. But gettin' back to the here and now, what—or who—are you afraid of?"

"Afraid? Is it that obvious?"

"Yeah, and it was from the moment you arrived."

"You're right, I am," she admitted with a heavy sigh, "but it's not a short story and it's late. Maybe we should wait until the morning."

"I won't sleep until I know what's goin' on. You said you were headed to Devlin's cabin. Start there. Who scared you so badly you had to ride up the mountain to get away?"

"Okay, I'll tell you, but you probably won't believe me," she declared, picking up her drink and taking a swallow. "It's Paul Darrow."

"Paul Darrow the trainer? What about him?"

"I think he's drugging horses at the show. At the beginning of the week I cut through one of the guest barns to save time and I saw him. At first I didn't give it a second thought, but his reaction when he spotted me—it was like I'd caught him robbing a bank. He turned beet red, then without any prodding from me, he said *I have to give him a shot for his allergies.*"

"That's odd," Clint mumbled.

"It was totally odd, but it gets worse. Just a couple of days ago I saw him go into another guest barn carrying an aluminum case. I—uh—I decided to follow him."

"You did what?"

"I admit when I was creeping down the barn aisle I felt like I shouldn't be there, but I couldn't stop myself."

"Damn, girl, I said it before and I'll say it again. You should have your butt spanked. I take it he saw you."

"Yeah."

As she'd mumbled her reply she'd lowered her gaze, and

Clint spotted a bright pink blush cross her face. Was it from guilt, or his implied threat?

"Anyway, I bolted out of there," she continued. "When I reached my car I was shaking like a leaf. I sat there for ages not sure what to do, and finally decided to drive over to Barney's trailer. I'm sure you must know Barney Harper, the show manager."

"Yep"

"I raced over there, only to find the door was locked, but when I started to leave I thought I heard voices."

"Please don't tell me you tried to listen."

"Uh, a bit more than that. I walked around to the back. There was an open window and I risked a peek. Paul was handing Barney a bunch of cash, then they started talking about what they'd do next."

"I can't believe this," Clint said, shaking his head. "What were you thinkin'?"

"I just wanted to know what was going on," she exclaimed, taking another drink. "Anyway, Barney suddenly cursed and said he'd forgotten to close the window. He turned around, but I don't think he saw me, and that's when I ran back to my car. I was climbing in when a guy on a motorbike rolled up and stopped right beside me. He sort of, glared at me through the car window. That's when I took off and went straight to the sheriff's office."

"That's the first sensible thing I've heard you say."

"Thanks, but it didn't do much good," she said with a frustrated frown. "The deputy behind the desk told me unless I knew which specific horses needed testing they couldn't do anything. Then I told him what I'd overheard, and he said it wasn't enough to act upon. All he did was promise to tell the security guards at the show to keep their eyes open. That was it."

"So…why did you head up to Devlin's cabin?"

"Last night I was out with some friends and I didn't get home until late. I drove into my garage, and when I got out of my car…"

"When you got out of your car, what?"

"The biker was there," she replied, her voice quivering.

"Inside your garage?" Clint exclaimed, staring at her wide-eyed.

"Uh-huh, and he walked right up to me. He must have followed me in," she said breathlessly. "Clint, I've never been so scared in my life. He told me if I said a word about anything I'd seen or heard—"

But she suddenly stopped speaking, and Clint saw a tear slip down her cheek.

"Tiffany, it's okay," he said, taking her hand. "How did he threaten you?"

"He said…I'd show up at the barn and find Molly dead. And it didn't end there."

CHAPTER FIVE

Tiffany's heart was thumping in her chest, and she couldn't stop the tears spilling from her eyes.

"What do you mean, it didn't end there," Clint asked quietly, moving an arm around her shoulders. "What else did he say? Did he hurt you?"

"Sorry…it was just so terrifying," she sputtered. "He grabbed me and pushed me up against the car and said it wasn't an idle threat. Then he shoved me to the ground and marched away. I was trembling so much I could barely make it inside. I would have called Matt Thompson, but he's away. Do you know him?"

"Sure, he and his wife Becky are friends of mine, along with the other folks around Lone Pine Hill. Devlin and Matilda Pike, and Callum and Kelly Coleman."

"Then you probably know Matt was a marine. He told me to call him if I ever had any problems, but like I said, he and Becky are gone. They're visiting her parents with the new baby. Then I thought about calling the sheriff's office, but I was too scared the biker would know somehow. I didn't know what to do."

"So that's why you went to your barn early this mornin' and rode Molly up to Devlin's cabin, but you were in such a panic you forgot your gloves—and anything else you might need—and lost your way," Clint said with a heavy frown.

"Uh…yes, but thank heavens I did, for both our sakes" she said earnestly, and for a fleeting moment she considered admitting she'd been searching for his cabin from the get-go. But she couldn't find the courage, and decided it didn't make any difference. "Devlin told me you had a cabin up here, and when I was listening to Paul and Barney outside the trailer, they talked about selling the merchandise they'd stolen from your stores. Does that make any sense?"

"Damn right it does!" Clint exclaimed. "There's been a rash of burglaries. Would you recognize this biker if you saw him again?"

"I'd know his face in a heartbeat. He has really bushy eyebrows, and his skin is rough."

"How tall do you think?"

"Well, in my garage he towered over me, so at least six feet."

"What color was his bike?"

"Black and silver, but I wouldn't know a Harley from a Honda."

"I'll send this information to my security people right away. Is there anything else you can tell me about him or what you overheard?"

"Let me think...the leather jacket and pants he was wearing looked weathered and old. Oh, his gloves! They were black with a red lightning bolt across the back. As far as what Barney and Paul were saying, once Barney started coming over to close the window I bolted. But Clint, what should I do? I can't stay here forever, and Elk Valley is a small community. Paul's barn isn't far from where I board Molly."

"Tiffany, tomorrow we're goin' into town and meetin' with the sheriff. You were assaulted and it has to be reported. That biker might be picked up for some other crime and he'll fit the description of your attacker."

"I hadn't thought of that, but we only have our horses here. I can't see riding down the mountain and back up again in one day."

"I'll have a jeep sent up in the mornin'. When we're finished with the sheriff we'll come right back."

"Clint, thank you, this is so kind of you."

"Hey, it sounds like you stumbled across the bastards who have been robbin' my stores. We know bikers are involved because of the security footage, but the license plates are covered just like their faces. We've had nothin' to go on."

"If the sheriff listens to me, maybe he'll bring Paul in for questioning and you can get more information."

"Trust me, he'll listen," Clint said solemnly, then frowning, he muttered, "Paul Darrow! Dammit to hell."

"I wish I knew what he's doing to the horses," Tiffany said angrily. "It's so upsetting. I need to call everyone and tell them to make sure the guest barns are being watched. Kelly and Callum are showing, and Devlin Pike will be giving performances on Merlin, but they'll hauling in and leaving when they're done so they should be okay. But I still need to warn them. Is there cell service up here?"

"I have a sat phone and internet, but you're better off callin' from your mobile when we're about halfway down the mountain tomorrow. The thing is, Tiffany, you don't know anything for sure. Choose your words carefully."

"Okay, but I wish I could alert the staff at the showgrounds."

"We'll leave that to the sheriff, but it's gettin' late," he replied, downing his drink and rising to his feet. "I don't know about you, but It's time for me to hit the hay."

"I'm feeling tired again too. Though I think that cognac might be making me a bit sleepy."

"It's taken the edge off," he said, reaching for her hand and helping her up. "A word of warnin'," he continued, staring down at her. "When I said you need your butt spanked, I meant it. No more takin' chances like you did or I'll do the honors."

"You wouldn't!"

The words had slipped from her lips before she could stop them. As he tilted his head to the side, the look in his eye made the butterflies in her stomach burst to life.

CHAPTER SIX

Clint couldn't quite believe she'd challenged him, and for a fleeting moment he thought he'd misheard. But a red flush was crawling across her face.

"You don't think so?" he retorted, tightening his hold around her waist.

"Well…uh…we just met."

"And your point is…?"

"I—uh—"

"Tiffany, you narrowly escaped gettin' your fingers burned real bad. If you haven't learned your lesson and you reach out and touch that hot stove again, yeah, I'll put you over my knee in a heartbeat. Or don't you think I'm a man of my word?"

"I'm sure you are," she stammered, "but like I said, we just met, I just don't think..."

"You don't think I would? How's this for starters?"

Deftly spinning her around, he landed several hard swats on her backside eliciting a sharp squeal, then swiftly jerked her back against his body.

"Now do you believe me?"

"What the fuck?" she panted, staring up at him with disbelief in her wide eyes.

"Cussin' won't help, and Tiffany, you opened that door."

"I did no such thing."

"Now you're just plain lyin, and lyin will get your ass bared and spanked real quick. You wanna rethink what you just said?"

"Uh…"

"You needed to know if I'm for real. That's why you made

that provocative remark. Now you have your answer. Right?"

"I guess..."

"You guess?"

"Okay, yes, you're right," she whispered.

With his cock surging to life, he slid his fingers into her hair and tugged back her head.

Her sapphire eyes sparkled up at him.

She was brave, brazen and beautiful.

An intoxicating combination.

Hot chemistry crackled between them, and though he ached to lean in and kiss her, she'd been right about one thing. They'd just met. But just as he was about to release her, she moved her arms around his neck.

"Clint...?"

"What ya doin'?"

"Please will you hold me for a second?"

Letting out a heavy sigh, he wrapped her into his arms, then closed his eyes and savored the feel of her body pressed against him.

"Thank you," she whispered. "I promise to be very careful from now on."

Not sure how to respond, he didn't say anything, but continued to hold her until he heard her yawn.

"It's time for some shut-eye," he said, pulling back. "You sleep well and I'll see you in the mornin'. By the way, I have business meetin's here. Your guest room is stocked with just about anything you might need."

"I thought that might be the case," she replied, stepping back and staring up at him. "Thanks, Clint, thanks for everything."

"I'm glad I was here. You get a good night's sleep."

"You too."

As she turned and walked away, he imagined slipping off her robe and admiring her naked body. Letting out a sigh and doing his best to ignore his stiffening cock, he moved into his office. The investigation into the burglaries was in the hands of his security team, but now a beautiful young woman had appeared out of nowhere and provided vital information. Picking up his phone, he placed a call to one of his assistants, a young man named Rudy White. It was late, but Clint paid him well and expected him to be available whenever he was needed.

"Good evening, Clint," Rudy said, answering in a sleepy voice.

"Hey, Rudy, send Jethro up here in a jeep tomorrow mornin', and I want it here by nine."

"Will do."

"What's goin' on with the security team and the store videos?"

"We've been trying get a better look at the three guys, but those ski masks make it almost impossible to see anything specific."

"Zoom in on their gloves. Look for a red lightnin' rod."

"Okay, sure will. Anything else?"

"That's it for the moment, thanks, Rudy. Goodnight."

"Goodnight, Clint."

Leaving his office and heading into the kitchen, Clint picked up the few dishes left on the table from Tiffany's dinner, washed and dried them and put them away. As he made his way down the hall to his bedroom, he could scarcely believe what Tiffany had overheard. The thefts had happened in stores in Dayville County, but Barney Harper and Paul Darrow were local to Elk Valley.

"Hey, Buck," he muttered, moving across to his dog stretched out on his furry bed in front of the low burning fire. "Life is full of surprises, isn't it buddy?"

Buck half-heartedly lifted his head, yawned and stretched, then laid it back down again.

"Yeah, I know, fella, I'm tired too."

Quickly undressing and climbing into bed, Clint closed his eyes, but his cock demanded attention. Pushing back the covers, he began to stroke himself, picturing the gorgeous girl in the room down the hall, naked and bent over his lap. He imagined her curvaceous backside turning bright pink from his slapping hand, and her pussy soaked when he pushed his finger into her channel.

As the surprisingly quick, powerful climax surged through his loins, he swallowed back his loud groans, then breathlessly reached for a handful of tissues from the nightstand.

"Damn," he mumbled as he let out a heavy sigh and closed his eyes. "What is it about her…?"

* * *

Though buzzed from the cognac, and still tired in spite of her afternoon nap, Tiffany couldn't sleep. All she could think about was the handsome cowboy just a hair's breath away.

Both Devlin and Matt had talked about the wealthy retailer and the fabulous home he'd built in the mountains. The idea of searching him out had been a tantalizing temptation, but after overhearing what she had, and the traumatic event in her garage, the exciting adventure to find him had changed.

Matt and Becky were away, and the sheriff's office ignored her plea for help. Tracking down Clint Kincaid had become imperative.

But there was more.

Much more.

And it was too soon to tell him.

She just hadn't realized how sexy and captivating he would be.

CHAPTER SEVEN

In his modest home located in the grounds of the barn he leased, Paul Darrow had stopped pouring the whiskey into a glass and was taking swigs straight from the bottle. He'd thought he'd come through the storm, but he feared disaster was lurking just around the corner.

His problems had started a couple of months before when the inevitable happened.

Many of the girls he'd trained had grown up, sold their horses and headed off to college. Those who stayed in Elk Valley had discovered boys, and spending time with them had become much more intriguing than being at the stable.

Not only had he lost his star students, new trainers had appeared. Callum and Kelly Coleman, the couple who had inherited Lone Pine Ranch, had expanded. Many of the horses they rehabilitated were now entering the show ring—and winning.

Devlin Pike, the daredevil rodeo rider, had also bought a property, and opened his doors to young riders—the very clients Paul believed should have come to him. He was the one with the proven track record.

Barely able to keep his head above water, desperate times called for desperate measures. At the latest horse show being held in Elk Valley, he had four students competing in different divisions. Each of them had a good shot at winning.

But a good shot wasn't a guarantee.

If he was to save his business, and demonstrate he was still the best in the area, he had to make sure they walked away with the blue ribbons and trophies. He had concocted a clear, but unscrupulous plan. Then to his horror, a couple of weeks before the first show, he was hit with an unexpected drama.

His truck died.

The truck that pulled his trailers.

He could arrange a hauler, but that was only a temporary fix, and picking up another one was impossible. Already up to his neck in credit card debt, he was unable to qualify for a vehicle loan, and he had no cash on hand.

He couldn't let people know how broke he was.

There was only one alternative.

His rough, tough, shady cousin, Dirk Griswald.

They'd been close as kids, but while Paul was drawn to a career working with horses, Dirk was all about making a quick buck, and he didn't care how. He lived in the criminal underworld, but in spite of their differences they'd remained friends.

Desperate for help, Paul had reluctantly called, and Dirk responded.

A couple of days later, he'd rolled into the barn driving a Ford F150 with his motorbike in the back. The gleaming black truck had only a few thousand miles on the odometer and looked brand new.

Paul knew better than to ask where it came from.

Then Dirk handed over an envelope with ten-thousand dollars in cash. When he explained what he wanted in return, Paul inwardly cringed, but Dirk had thrown him a lifeline and he had to do his cousin's bidding.

Paul sat with his criminal cousin studying the Kincaid Western Wear, Tack and Feed website. He'd pointed out the most expensive boots, show clothing, bridles, bits, halters and other items. Then he'd visited the stores in Dayville County and surreptitiously photographed the displays, the exits, the back of the store, the windows in the men's and women's restrooms, and the security cameras inside and out. As far as Paul was concerned, once he'd handed Dirk the information, his debt has been paid.

Now the show was underway, and his students had qualified to enter the next level of competition.

It was time to pull out the needles.

It was risky as hell and no fun.

Barney Harper, the show ground's manager, would be overseeing the random drug testing, and Paul had to make sure certain horses were excluded. Barney had accepted a bribe, but to make sure Barney wouldn't ask for more money, Paul had asked Dirk to pay him a threatening visit.

Everything went according to plan, but out of the blue, it was going to hell in a hay basket, and Paul was beside himself.

Tiffany Sullivan had walked past a stall while he was injecting a horse. Instead of smiling and saying hello, he'd panicked. His face had turned beet red, and he'd blurted out a story about the horse having allergies.

A short time later, when he'd been handing the last of the bribe money to Barney, Paul had spotted her by an open window. She had ducked out of sight, but he had no idea how much she had overheard.

Then Dirk had arrived, and Paul had made a fatal error.

He'd mentioned his concerns about Tiffany.

When Dirk had demanded to know where Tiffany lived, Barney hastily pulled up her address on his computer. Marching from the trailer, Dirk had jumped on his bike and sped off.

Now Tiffany had disappeared.

All Paul could do was pray the young woman was okay.

His criminal cousin was capable of just about anything.

Downing another swig of whiskey and staring out at the night sky, Paul knew he was in over his head.

CHAPTER EIGHT

When Tiffany opened her eyes the following morning, her first thoughts were about Molly. Picking up her phone from the nightstand she discovered it was almost eight o'clock, and immediately wondered if her mare had been fed.

Hastily climbing from bed, she took a quick shower, pulled on the clothes she'd left in a heap on the floor, and hurried down the hall. Finding the kitchen empty, she stepped outside and walked across to the barn.

But she'd neglected to put on her jacket.

Shivering as she entered, she found the door leading out to the attached corral had been opened. Stepping into the stall and moving closer, she saw Molly was blanketed and happily munching a flake of hay.

"Molly, are you okay, girl?"

The mare jerked up her head, nickered, and ambled forward.

"I'm sorry, I don't have any treats," Tiffany murmured as she stroked her horse's neck.

"I do!"

Turning around, she saw Clint striding towards her.

"Here are some carrots," he said with a grin, breaking them in half.

As Tiffany offered them to Molly, the mare gobbled them up, then Clint's horse poked his head over the top of the fence.

"Don't worry, Leroy, I have some for you too," Clint said with a grin.

"She seems happy," Tiffany remarked, feeling a wave of relief as she stepped out of the cold air and back into the barn.

"Where's your jacket?" Clint asked, following her.

"I was in such a hurry I forgot to put it on."

"You'd better get in the house, and what you were wearing when you arrived isn't warm enough for where we are. You must've been freezin' when you were riding up here yesterday."

"I started feeling it around the halfway point," she said as they walked quickly across the drive and into the kitchen. But as she opened the door she heard the sound of an approaching car.

"That'll be Jethro," Clint declared. "He works in one of my warehouses and helps with my horses when I need it. You don't have to worry about your mare. He'll stay here while we go into town. Help yourself to breakfast while I talk to him. There's cereal in the cupboard and the coffee pot is full."

Before she could thank him, he marched away, and she paused to admire his wide shoulders and strong stride.

Clint Kincaid was a force to be reckoned with.

* * *

Clint instructed Jethro to keep his eyes open and stay alert. The rough biker who had attacked Tiffany may have found out she'd left on her mare, and might decide to check out the mountain trails. Returning to the house, he found Tiffany enjoying a bowl of instant oatmeal.

"I have a down jacket you can have," he said, pouring himself a mug of coffee. "You'll need it bein' up here. I've already called the sheriff and he's expectin' us. We'll leave as soon as you're ready."

"I'm ready now," she exclaimed, rising to her feet.

"No you're not. Finish your oatmeal and I'll dig out that jacket."

Taking his mug with him, he headed down the hall to a large

walk-in closet where he kept samples and merchandise to give as gifts to visiting VIPs. The aqua down jacket was longer than he remembered, but had a zipper that could slide up from the bottom as well as down from the top, which made it ideal for riding. Carrying it back to the kitchen, he found her washing out the bowl.

"Oh, wow, Clint, that's gorgeous," she exclaimed as she turned around. "Are you sure you don't mind me borrowing it?"

"Tiffany, it's yours."

"But it's—"

"Warm and you can wear it in the saddle," he interjected. "I'm pretty good at guessin' sizes, and you're a six, or a small. Right?"

"Yes, I am."

"It should fit you perfectly," he continued, tearing off the plastic and sliding down the zipper. "Try it on."

As he held it open, she turned around and slid her arms down the sleeves.

"Yep, fit's just like I thought it would," he exclaimed, stepping in front of her. "Looks like it's tailor made for you, and the color looks great."

"This is wonderful. It's so light but so comfortable and cozy. Thank you."

Suddenly, to his surprise, she threw her arms around his neck and hugged him.

"Thank you for everything."

As he hugged her back, he closed his eyes and breathed her in. But the luscious feel of her body pressed against his was shooting energy through his loins and he quickly released her.

"You're welcome, but we need to get outta here. I promised the sheriff we'd be at his office before ten."

"It's so weird about Paul," she remarked as they walked outside. "I don't know him well, but he has a terrific reputation and some top riders. It's hard to believe he's involved with someone like that biker."

"Get in and I'll tell you what I know about Paul Darrow," he declared, opening the Jeep's door.

"That doesn't sound good."

"It's not!"

As she climbed into the passenger seat, he strode around the vehicle and settled behind the wheel.

"Tiffany, Paul Darrow is in a financial mess," Clint declared, starting up the Jeep and rolling down the drive. "The store manager here in Elk Valley kept givin' him credit. When I ran a check I discovered he'd maxed out his credit cards and was fallin' behind on his payments. I had to put my foot down and cut him off. That was a couple of months ago, and he still hasn't paid a dime against his account."

"But he has one of the top barns in the area."

"How many people does he have at the show?"

"Now that I think about it, only four that I know of. A bunch of his kids went off to college, but I know he sold some horses. He would have made a bunch of money from them."

"He was probably behind with his feed bill or barn lease payments. Regardless, that man is sinkin' fast."

CHAPTER NINE

As Clint drove carefully down the mountain, Tiffany called Callum and told him she'd witnessed Paul Darrow injecting a horse in one of the guest barns.

"Maybe he was doing someone a favor," she suggested, "I don't know, but it struck me as odd and I wanted to let you know."

"Thanks, Tiffany, and I'll give Devlin a heads up. We can't be too careful. I ran into Paul the other day and he wasn't his usual cheery self. Something is definitely up with him. I guess I'll see you at the show grounds."

"Uh, actually, I'm canceling my classes and taking a break."

"Okay, well, thanks, Tiffany. Take care."

"You're welcome," she said, then ending the call, she let out a heavy sigh. "There, done, I hope I sounded normal."

"You did, and you handled that perfectly," Clint assured her, then pointed towards his left. "See that huge, rounded boulder, that's where you turn to go up to Devlin's cabin. The trail becomes evident just a short distance past it."

"That's right, I remember now," she lied, and feeling a ripple of guilt, she decided she'd tell him the truth as soon as the right opportunity presented itself.

"If you want to listen to some music there should be some CD's in the glove compartment," he suggested. "Probably all country artists, though."

"I love country!"

Grateful for the distraction, she found Jason Aldean's latest release and slipped the disc into the player.

For the remainder of the drive she sat back and enjoyed the music, smiling when sexy, suggestive lyrics filled the air. But when they drove through town, she kept watch for the black and silver motorbike. By the time Clint parked at the Sheriff's station, she was a bundle of nerves.

"Why am I so worried?" she muttered, her pulse racing as they walked across the parking lot.

"Because you've been threatened, and it was scary as hell," Clint replied, moving his arm around her shoulders. "But I'm here, and the sheriff will know how to deal with this—all of it—Paul, the biker, Barney, everything."

Though she wanted to believe him, an uncomfortable churning rolled through her stomach. Walking through the doors, she was relieved to see the deputy behind the counter was not the one who had brushed her off, and they waited only a couple of minutes before an attractive woman led them through to meet the sheriff.

"Thanks for seein' us," Clint said as they sat in front of his desk.

"No problem, Clint. I know you wouldn't be here if it wasn't important. What can I do for you?"

"This is Tiffany Sullivan," Clint continued. "She recently saw and heard some things she shouldn't have, then was attacked and threatened in her garage."

"It's nice to meet you, Miss Sullivan, and that's dreadful, but I must ask, why didn't you report this at the time?"

"I did," she exclaimed, "but the deputy out front said I didn't have enough evidence."

"Are you sayin' you came in right after this happened and you were told we couldn't help you?"

"Yes, I didn't know where to turn or what to do."

"Sheriff, Tiffany was so scared she rode her horse up the mountain to hide out in Devlin Pike's cabin. But she lost her way and found me instead."

"Miss Sullivan—" the sheriff began.

"Please call me Tiffany."

"Tiffany, I cannot tell you how sorry I am. Rest assured I'll find out who was on duty at the time and they will be corrected. Please, tell me everything."

* * *

As Tiffany relayed her story the sheriff listened without comment, then promising to return momentarily, he excused himself and left the room.

"You see," Clint said softly, taking her hand, "I told you he'd take you seriously."

"Thank goodness," she replied, swallowing back the heat in her throat. "Except—what if that biker finds out I've reported him?"

But before Clint could reply, the sheriff returned and handed her a photograph.

"Is this the man who attacked you?"

"Yes," she exclaimed, staring at the picture, "that's him, that's definitely him. Who is he?"

"His name is Dirk Griswald, and we've been after him for a while," the sheriff replied, returning to sit behind his desk. "I even received a call from the Feds. They have a field agent here tryin' to track him down. I'll let them know about this, and I'll also contact Sheriff Henderson in Dayville County."

"Something just occurred to me," Clint said thoughtfully. "The thieves target only the expensive items, and from what we've seen on the videos, they know exactly where they are. That's why they're in and out so fast. I thought they must have someone on the inside, but this could be where Paul Darrow fits in. He would know the expensive, popular items, and he could wander around without drawin' any attention."

"I'll have him and Barney Harper picked up right away, and I'll put out an APB on Griswald. Tiffany, I know it's scary when you've been threatened, and I'm sorry you didn't get the help you needed when you first came to us. Is there somewhere you can stay for a little while?"

"Up at my cabin," Clint said quickly. "She and her horse will be safe there."

"Good. Make sure you give my secretary all your contact information, and I'll be in touch as soon as I have any news. If you remember anything else, or need me, don't hesitate to call."

"Thank you, Sheriff,' Tiffany said gratefully, rising to her feet and shaking his hand. "I appreciate this very much."

"That's what I'm here for. Bye, Clint, I'm glad you came in."

As they left the sheriff's office and walked outside, Tiffany felt relieved. But the specter of the brutish thug looming over her suddenly flashed through her mind. Stopping abruptly, she stared up and down the street.

"What is it?" Clint asked. "Did you just notice something?"

"No, I guess I'm just being paranoid. I was looking to see if there was a motorcycle parked anywhere."

"Nope, none in sight."

"I was going to ask if we could swing by my place so I can pack a few things, but I'm not sure it would be safe."

"Hey, you're with me, you'll be fine, and before we go back up the mountain I'll stop at Matilda's Munchies for some of her delicious desserts."

"I love her Australian cookies—or biscuits as she calls them."

"They're delicious, and don't worry, I'll keep a close watch to make sure we're not bein' followed when we head out of town."

"Now I'm making you paranoid," she said with a sigh as they reached the jeep.

"Bein' paranoid isn't necessarily a bad thing," he replied,

giving her a quick hug, then opened her door.

Neither of them paid any attention to an old, white sedan with tinted windows parked nearby.

CHAPTER TEN

Driving up to Tiffany's house, Clint eyeballed the street. There were no motorbikes to be seen, and nothing seemed out of the ordinary. As he turned into her driveway, she opened the garage door with her remote control. It was empty. She'd left her car at the barn where she boarded Molly when she'd started off on the mountain trek.

"Are you okay," he asked softly as he rolled inside.

"My pulse is racing a bit, but yeah, I'm okay."

"I'm here, and it's just you and me. You can close the garage and relax."

Shifting in her seat and looking back, she pressed the remote and the door rolled down behind them.

"Better?" he asked.

"Yes, better, thank you," she replied, then letting out a sigh, she climbed out. But entering the house, she suddenly stood stock still in the middle of the kitchen looking like a deer in headlights.

"Tiffany? What's wrong?"

"It's just weird being back here. Everything seems so normal, like nothing happened, but it has. How the hell did I make it up that mountain? Poor Molly. What a wonderful horse she is."

"She's strong and in great shape," he said reassuringly. "She probably loved every minute."

"Clint...thank you for rescuing us."

Staring at her pretty but anguished face, he suddenly realized how much he wanted her.

And not just in his bed.

He wanted to be around her dazzling smile and sparkling eyes.

He wanted to spank her ass for being so reckless.

He wanted to protect her from harm and make her feel safe.

Unable to stop himself, he strode forward and wrapped her into his arms.

"Believe me, it was my pleasure," he murmured, holding her tightly.

"I was so scared, and the truth is, there's a part of me that thinks that monster will show up again."

"It's understandable," he whispered, then sliding his fingers into her hair, he tugged back her head. "Think about this instead."

Leaning in and pressing his lips against hers, he kissed her softly, then urgently, demanding her response. As she pressed her body against him, he tightened his grip on her hair and devoured her mouth. With his cock surging to life in his jeans, he slid his hand down her back and gripped her backside.

"I wanna kiss every part of you," he murmured, his lips at her ear, "and spank you for sneakin' behind that trailer, then make love to you."

"Clint, I want you to do all those things..."

Feeling her longing and passionate need, he swiftly swept her up, marched from the kitchen and found himself in a comfortable lounge.

"The hall, turn left," she whispered.

Carrying her across the room and through to the passage, he immediately saw the open door to her bedroom. Striding forward, he kicked it shut with his foot, though he wasn't sure why, then laid her on the bed. The shades were closed over the window, filling the room with a soft, dim light.

As he pulled off his sweater and shirt, to his surprise and delight she followed suit, lifting her fuzzy, long-sleeved sweatshirt over her head. Swiftly removing his belt and boots, he dropped his jeans, then turned his attention back to her. Pulling off her boots, he unzipped the stretch denim riding pants and shimmied them down her legs, jerking them off and tossing them aside. Pausing for a moment, he stood over her and admired her luscious body.

"Tiffany, you're gorgeous," he breathed, leaning over her.

A frown crinkled her brow.

"And you—" she murmured, running her fingertips across his biceps and chest. "You're so strong...and so..."

"What?"

"Just strong, all of you, inside and out."

Grinning, he stretched out beside her, deftly unsnapped her bra, slid it down her arms and let it drop on the floor. As he lowered his lips to her nipples, she raised her chest to meet his mouth, letting out soft moans and whimpers.

"Clint, I want you so much."

"I want you too," he crooned, moving his lips to nuzzle her neck as he shoved his hand between her legs. "I want you like crazy."

Swiftly removing her underwear, he pulled off his boxers, then rested his weight on top of her and pinned her wrists on either side of her head.

"I've got you now," he growled, lowering his mouth to her neck to suck in her skin.

As she cried out and squirmed beneath him, he traveled his vampire kiss down her chest and back to her breasts, hungrily drawing in her cherry tips one after the other. His hardness was pressed against her, and her urgent writhing continued to send energy through his loins. Finally straightening up, he rolled her onto her stomach, spread her legs, then kneeled between them and pulled up her hips.

"Now I'm gonna redden your backside," he warned gruffly,

landing two quick slaps. “Tell me why.”

“Oooh, Clint,” she whimpered, though salaciously wiggling her hips.

“Tell me!” he demanded, spanking her again.

“Because I took chances I shouldn’t have,” she wailed. “I won’t do that again.”

“Nope, you won’t,” he said sternly, smacking her cheeks one after the other. “Your ass is so spankable,” he grunted, continuing to smack without pause. “Fair warnin’, you can expect more of the same if you stick around.”

Abruptly placing his rigid rod at her entrance, he thrust inside her slick wetness, eliciting a loud cry. With her earnest wails echoing through his head, he clutched her waist and accelerated, stroking for long, thrilling minutes, then staying buried inside her, he stopped and slipped a hand beneath her.

“How sensitive is your clit,” he muttered, leaning over her and kissing her neck. “If I rub it hard enough will you come?”

“Yes,” she bleated breathlessly. “I will. I’m so close.”

“Put your finger where mine is and rub yourself while I fuck you.”

Turning her head to the side, she dropped her shoulder onto the pillow and moved her hand to her pussy. As she began to rub, he straightened up, gripped her hips, and guided by her whimpers and cries, he resumed his fervent thrusting. When he sensed she was nearing her climax he slowed down. But she was already on the verge.

“Please, Clint, please don’t stop. I’m there, I’m there!”

“Then come for me!”

Gritting his teeth, he quickened his pace.

Her body shuddered, and as she cried out her euphoric joy his release seized him. Groaning loudly and swiftly pulling out, he exploded over her gloriously red backside.

CHAPTER ELEVEN

With her head resting against Clint's chest, Tiffany listened to the steady rhythm of his heart, and relished the feel of his muscled arm around her. She never expected they would end up making love in her bedroom. His beautiful mountain home perhaps. It was so romantic. Yet he was there, she was with him, and she never wanted the sublime moment to end.

She sighed, and a soft smile curled her lips. They'd be leaving soon, but she was sure they would share many more magic moments in his cabin, though the word *cabin* wasn't exactly accurate for the luxury retreat.

"Damn, how long have I been asleep?" he mumbled, stirring beside her and breaking into her thoughts.

"I'm not sure. I just woke up myself. I thought I heard the front door open. It sort of squeaks, but that's just ridiculous—or is it?" she added urgently, suddenly worried she may not have imagined it.

"No, it's not," he whispered, quickly climbing from the bed.

Pulling on his boxers and jeans, he stepped up to the bedroom door and slowly turned the handle. Watching him with her heart in her mouth, she suddenly realized her phone was in her jacket in the Jeep.

"Someone's walkin' around out there. I can hear your creaky floorboards" he whispered. "Dammit, my phone's in the Jeep."

"Mine is too."

"Is your closet a walk-in?" he asked softly, hastily returning to the bed.

"Yes."

"Go into the bathroom and turn on the shower, then run into your closet and hide behind your clothes. Don't turn the light on, and no matter what you hear, stay put. Got it?"

"Okay."

"Go."

Her heart racing a mile a minute, she dashed into the bathroom, turned on the shower faucets, then grabbed her robe off its hook and wrapped it around her body as she hurried into her closet. But knowing she wouldn't be seen in the dark space, she left the door open a crack and peered through the tiny space.

Clint was standing behind the bedroom door with his back to the wall. She guessed he would jump on whoever walked in. Saying a heartfelt prayer, she held her breath and waited.

* * *

The sound of the shower had worked, and Clint listened intently to the approaching footfalls. As the door slowly opened, he lowered his gaze and saw a man's heavy boot, then the intruder's hand fall away from the handle.

Suddenly slamming the hard, wooden door against the unsuspecting villain, Clint heard a shocked wail, then swiftly stepping around, he landed a fierce punch in the brute's gut. As the man doubled over and tumbled down, a gun clattered against the hardwood floor. Snatching it up, Clint stuffed it into the back of his jeans, then hastily straddled the groaning crook and yanked his hands behind his back.

"Here, you can tie him with these!"

Jerking his head up, he found Tiffany hurrying towards him holding several scarves. Wordlessly grabbing one, he deftly bound the thug's wrists together, then quickly taking a second, he followed suit with the man's ankles, leaving a tail long enough to hogtie him.

"Turn on the light," Clint said sharply, yanking back the criminal's head to study his injuries. But as she flicked the wall switch she let out a sharp cry.

"Clint! It's him! It's Dirk Griswald."

"Fuck," Dirk snarled, glaring up at them. "You'll both fuckin' pay for this."

Ignoring the comment, Clint deftly checked Dirk's pockets, finding a wallet stuffed with cash, but no phone. Rising to his feet, he lifted the gun from his waistband and peered into the hall. Seeing no-one, he stepped cautiously into the living room. There wasn't a sound, and the front door was closed.

"Tiffany, is there another bedroom?" he asked, hurrying back to her.

"Yes, it's the next door down the hall."

"Does it have a lock?"

"It does."

"Grab whatever you need and get changed there, then stay put until I come and get you. I'm going out to the Jeep to call the sheriff. I'll be right back."

"But Dirk is tied up. Can't I just get dressed and come with you?"

"Do as I say," he said sternly. "Get your things, and hurry."

While she gathered together clean clothes, he made sure there was no-one else lurking in the small home, then hurried back to find her stepping around Dirk and moving into the hall. Turning out the bedroom light, Clint closed the door and walked her down to the second bedroom.

"Remember, stay here until I come and get you," he repeated as they entered. "And this time do as you're told. Understood?"

"Yes, Clint, sorry, I—"

"We'll talk about it later."

"Please don't be mad."

"I'm not, but you can be difficult sometimes," he replied, then kissing her quickly, he hurried into the garage and made the call. To his great relief, the sheriff picked up and promised to be there with squad cars right away.

Letting out a heavy, relieved breath, Clint said a quick prayer of thanks, then strode back into the house to fetch Tiffany. When she opened the door, she stared up at him with wide eyes.

"Clint...you were amazing," she breathed. "You handled that guy like a pro."

"He may be big and look tough, but he's an idiot," Clint replied, taking her into his arms. "The sheriff will be here any minute and this whole mess will be cleared up. And before you ask, even though Dirk will be locked up, I want you to come back to the cabin with me. I'm sure he'll have friends."

"I'd like that very much," she said softly, then breaking into a grin, she added, "I can't leave Molly."

"You are soooo sassy."

"Yeah, well, that's one of my best qualities."

"And spankin' sassy backsides is one of mine."

CHAPTER TWELVE

After the deputies arrested Dirk Griswald, Tiffany returned to the bedroom and packed a bag, while the sheriff took Clint into the kitchen for a private conversation.

"Paul Darrow and Barney Harper were picked up and they're both talkin', especially Paul," the sheriff declared. "He'll do anything to escape prison, or at least lower his sentence. He's already admitted to givin' Dirk information about your stores."

"Unbelievable," Clint muttered. "Will he serve time?"

"He's already tryin' to make a deal, but I'll keep you posted. Right now you and Tiffany need to come back to the station to give your statements about what happened here. Then you can return to that mountain home of yours and catch your breath."

"Thanks, Sheriff, I'm lookin' forward to it. What are the chances of recoverin' my stolen merchandise?"

"Hard to say at this point. I don't know if Griswald has moved it on to another party or if it's stashed some place. I'll do my best to find out."

"I'm ready," Tiffany declared, walking up to join them carrying a small suitcase.

"Thanks, Sheriff, we'll see you shortly," Clint said, shaking his hand.

"Clint, why will we see him shortly," she asked as Clint took her suitcase and they headed to the garage.

"We need to stop at the station and give our statements."

"Oh, of course. On our way back to the mountain I'd like to swing by and see Gwen if that's okay."

"Gwen?"

"She's the woman who owns the small barn where I keep Molly."

"Sure, no problem," Clint replied as they climbed into the Jeep.

"Gwen's a character," Tiffany remarked with a grin. "She's kind of loony, but she's really sweet. Anyway, she's probably worried about me, and I want to see how she's doing with her problem child, though I doubt there's much change in just a couple of days."

"Problem child?" Clint asked as he backed out of the garage and started down the street.

"She adopted a paint. His name is Oreo. He's hard to catch and I'm worried she's in over her head."

"Hmmm, if she's open to suggestions—"

"I'm sure she would be. She's had him almost a month and he looks a whole lot better, but she hasn't made much headway handling him."

"He sounds like a candidate for Devlin or Callum. I know Devlin has room, and if she wants to keep the horse at her property Devlin would be willing to go there. I don't think Callum would. Regardless, I'll take a gander and see if I can give her some suggestions."

"So...you train?"

"I used to, but after I opened my first store and realized I could expand, I had to make a choice. Trainin' or the retail business. There's a whole lot more money and room for growth in retail. I've never looked back, but I do miss workin' with horses. I'd like to help if I can."

"Clint, that would be great, thank you," she said gratefully as they rolled into the station parking lot, but as he came to a stop, her phone rang. Lifting it from her bag, she glanced at the screen. "I need to take this. Can I meet you inside?"

"Sure, but don't be too long."

"I won't, it's just mom."

"I'd love to hear about your family," he said quickly, then climbed from the Jeep and strode up to the entrance.

But it bothered him he knew nothing about her.

He wasn't surprised her home was modest, but the garage had been empty. Most people—himself included—used their garage for storage, and he hadn't seen a single box.

He turned and stared back at her. She was still on the phone, but she smiled and waved. He waved back, then walked through the heavy doors and up to the deputy behind the counter to check in.

As he sat down to wait, his deep pondering continued. He'd have plenty of time to learn about her when they returned to his home, but his curiosity was growing. Lifting out his phone, he texted Ken Baker, the head of his security team.

Ken, send me background information on Tiffany Sullivan. She currently lives at 35 Maple Avenue in Elk Valley. It's probably a rental. Occupation and DOB unknown.

His finger hovered over the send button.

"Mr. Kincaid?" Darting his head up, he saw Marilyn, the sheriff's secretary, walking towards him. "Do you want to come in and give your statement, or wait for your friend?"

Glancing out the door, he spotted Tiffany walking across the parking lot.

"She's on her way," he replied, deleting the message and dropping his phone back in his pocket.

"Sorry to keep you waiting," Tiffany said to Marilyn as she entered, then shot Clint a warm smile.

"You didn't," Marilyn replied. "Follow me."

"Is everything okay, Tiffany," he asked softly.

"Yes, fine, but I can't wait to get this over with. I want to see

Gwen and get back to Molly."

"How long have you boarded with her?"

"Only about four months. Like I said, it's a small barn, but I really like it."

"If I had to board I'd prefer small over big," he remarked, but before he could continue the conversation, Marilyn was ushering them into an office where a deputy was waiting to take their statements.

CHAPTER THIRTEEN

It didn't take long to give their statements, and Clint was soon following Tiffany's directions to the small facility where she boarded Molly. During the drive he began to ask questions, and learned Tiffany was a realtor.

"I'd been wanting to get out of the city, and when I visited Becky to check out Elk Valley her father offered me a job selling homes in his new development. I loved the community, but not the work. It wasn't for me."

"Why? Doesn't a situation like that offer security?"

"Yes, but it was basically pencil pushing. I like helping people get their homes ready for sale with staging and decorating, and there was none of that with the Clarkson houses. Besides that, I'm used to selling all kinds of interesting places. Everything from Victorian mansions to sleek contemporaries. That was part of the fun."

"I see what you mean," Clint remarked as they drove into Gwen's barn. "What's the name of this place? I don't see a sign anywhere."

"She doesn't have one, a name I mean, but that's Gwen. I told you, she's a character."

As he came to a stop and they climbed from the Jeep, Clint was glad he hadn't sent the text to his security chief. Tiffany was a realtor. It made sense. She had the personality and the brains, and he was looking forward to discovering more about her the right way. By talking and spending time together.

"Tiffany, I'm so happy to see you," a female voice called. "How are you? How's Molly?"

Looking across to the barn, he spied a woman dressed in jeans and a billowing blouse hurrying towards them. She was of average height and weight, but she had long, greying blonde hair piled haphazardly on top of her head. He guessed her to be somewhere north of forty.

"Hi, Gwen," Tiffany said happily. "We're both great. Sorry I haven't been in touch, things have been a bit crazy. This is Clint Kincaid. Clint, this is Gwen Mitchell."

"Oh, my stars!" Gwen exclaimed, grabbing his hand and shaking it earnestly. "I love your stores. It's such an honor to meet you."

"It's good to meet you too," he replied with a chuckle. "Tiffany said you have a new horse that can be a bit difficult."

"A bit?" she said, rolling her eyes. "I'm beside myself. I love him to pieces, but, my stars," she repeated, "what a handful he is. It's strange though. He lets me blanket him and he's so sweet, but I can't get the darn halter on. I just don't know what to do."

"I've done a little trainin' in my time. Would you like me to—"

"Lord, yes," she said excitedly. "I know all about your training background. I read an article in Western Wear magazine. You had champions and you had to choose between horses and your business. That must have been very difficult."

"Yeah, I was just tellin' Tiffany about it."

"I'd love some advice about Oreo when you have the time."

"I have the time right now."

"You do? Oh my stars! He's in his corral. I'll try to get his halter on and you can see for yourself."

She started walking quickly into the barn, and Tiffany looped her arm around his as they followed.

"See," she whispered with a wink.

"I do," he replied, smiling broadly, "but I like her."

Entering the barn, he found it surprisingly organized, and

Gwen was standing outside a stall holding a halter and lead rope.

"He's through here," she declared, waving them over, "in the attached corral."

"Go ahead," Clint called back. "We'll watch from the stall."

"But he might try to run back in. He does that sometimes."

"Don't worry about us. Just do what you normally would and I'll take it from there."

"Okay, if you're sure."

"I'm sure."

She disappeared, and as they reached the oversized stall, again he was impressed. The shavings were clean and the water buckets sparkled. Walking through to the door that led outside, he was pleased to find the corral extended a fair distance, and glancing down either side of the barn, he noticed three other corrals offered the same space.

"Are you ready to watch me?" Gwen called from the middle of the corral, pointing at the paint standing at the far end.

"He's a beauty," Clint remarked. "Go ahead, let me see what he does."

Taking a deep breath, Gwen pulled a treat from her pocket and began walking up to her horse.

"Here's an apple snack," she offered, extending her hand as she approached.

Oreo moved over to her and gobbled up the treat, but as soon as she lifted the halter he turned and trotted away.

"See?" she called. "If I loop the rope around his neck he does the same thing and that's scary."

Ambling forward, Clint took the halter and rope from her hands.

"Go on back to Tiffany. If you're worried close the bottom half of the door and stand behind it."

"Oh, I will, believe me," she replied. "Do you want a treat?"

"No thanks, and Oreo doesn't need one either," he said, then laughed out loud at his own joke. It was contagious and she started giggling. "Relax, Gwen. I think I can help."

"Really?"

"No promises, but I'll give it a shot."

"Oh my stars, thank you."

"I haven't done anything yet."

"But at least you're willing to try. I've had a couple of people over and they didn't even want to do that. I guess that's why he was at the rescue place."

"Probably. Join Tiffany behind the door and I'll get to work."

"Thank you again," she exclaimed, then hurried back to the stall.

Waiting until she was settled, he turned his attention to the gelding already eyeing him.

"We're gonna have a little talk," Clint declared, slowly walking towards him, "but I'll be speakin' your language, and you won't have any trouble understandin' me."

CHAPTER FOURTEEN

The horse didn't move, but Clint wasn't surprised. Gwen was hyper, and her energy was part of the problem. As he neared he slowed his step, then stopped. Oreo snorted. It was a good sign.

"Hey, big boy," Clint said softly, keeping the halter and lead rope loosely at his side.

Not seeing any signs of nervousness or fear, he stepped forward and placed his hand firmly on Oreo's withers. The horse turned its head and stared back at him.

"I bet you've got plenty of stories to tell," Clint remarked, looking him in the eye. "You're a smart fella. Let's see what you know." Moving towards Oreo's rear, Clint raised the rope in his right hand, pointed forward with his left, and clucked. "Go on now."

Immediately the horse started walking away, and Clint stayed with him, encouraging him to keep moving. When a minute or so had passed, Clint abruptly strode in front of him, and asked him turn and walk the other way. The horse did exactly as Clint directed. The pair continued to amble calmly around the corral, with Clint occasionally changing direction. When he felt the time was right, he lowered both arms and moved backwards.

Oreo tossed his head, then followed him.

When Clint stopped, Oreo walked up and stood in front of him.

"Yep, that's what I figured," Clint said, letting out a sigh as he stroked the horse's neck.

Lifting the halter, he slid it over Oreo's head without any

issues, attached the lead rope, and walked him into the center of the corral.

"Ready for the next bit?" he asked, raising the tail of the rope and gently twirling it towards the horse's flank.

Oreo moved his back feet, then stopped.

Clint walked to his other side and repeated the exercise.

"Time to say hello to your mom, and you be nice, ya hear?" As Oreo snorted and shook his head, Clint chuckled. "Yeah, I know, but try," he said quietly, then looked across at Gwen who was staring in shock. The horse was smart and easy. Gwen was the problem. "Come on out here, Gwen. Be calm and walk slowly."

"Calm and slow," she repeated. "Okay, I'll try, but I'm so excited."

"Then stay there until you're not."

"Oh, my stars!"

Clint was about to turn his attention back to the handsome gelding when he saw Tiffany say something to the overjoyed woman. A moment later, Gwen opened the stall door and strolled towards them.

"Clint, how on earth did you do that?" she asked as she reached him.

"Horses are extremely sensitive. They pick up on your energy," Clint replied. "If you're hyper, or nervous, or worried, they will be too. I was calm and confident. Horses also need their humans to lead the way. That doesn't mean bully them, it means showin' them what you want. Not take this lead rope and walk him around the corral. Stay calm and talk to him, tell him about your favorite book or movie. If he pesters you for a treat, refuse. When you're ready, stop and back him up, then go forward again. Let him know you're in charge."

"Wow, okay."

"Remember, calm and confident."

"Got it. Calm and confident."

"I'll be watchin' with Tiffany. If you need me, wave me over."

"Thank you so much," she said earnestly. "I was at my wits end."

"You're welcome. Now take your handsome boy for a walk."

As Clint headed back to the stall, he knew the woman had been near tears. She'd only had Oreo a short time, but it was obvious she had already developed a deep attachment.

"That was impressive," Tiffany said as he joined her.

"Not really, just basic stuff, but she does need help. I'll contact Devlin for her. What?" he asked as Tiffany continued to stare up at him.

"You were so good with Oreo, and you're helping a complete stranger. Not everyone would do that. And look what you've done for me."

"I'll never turn my back on a horse in need, and Tiffany, when you showed up at my house you were exhausted and the sun was settin'. I couldn't possibly turn you away."

"I'm feeling very lucky to know you," she murmured, stepping closer to him, "especially after everything that's happened. Thank you."

"You've already thanked me," he said, then taking a breath, he added, "I'm sorry you had to deal with all the crap, but it sure has worked out well, don't ya think?"

"Yes, it has," she replied, breaking into a smile and leaning against his chest.

"Look, Gwen's doin' really well, but I'd better call Devlin now. When I get home I need to speak with my security people and bring them up to speed."

"While you're doing that I'll pack up Molly's supplements. I left in such a hurry I didn't grab anything. If you need me I'll be through there," she said, pointing to a nearby door.

"Wait, before you go. What did you say to Gwen? It worked a

treat."

"I told her she and Oreo aren't alone anymore and she can relax."

* * *

As Clint grinned and lifted his phone from his back pocket, Tiffany walked across the barn aisle to the feed room. But once inside, she sat on the edge of a grain container and dropped her head in her hands.

She was crazy about him.

Not because he was the wealthy, well-known Clint Kincaid.

But because he was brave and smart and strong.

And he made her toes curl and filled her heart.

But she'd lied, and he was bound to find out the truth.

She needed to come clean before things went any further. She owed him that much…and a whole lot more.

"I'm falling in love with him," she mumbled, shaking her head.

The door creaked.

Darting her eyes up, she found Clint moving towards her.

CHAPTER FIFTEEN

Tiffany caught her breath.

What had Clint heard?

She was trying to think of something to say when he suddenly stepped forward, grabbed her hand and pulled her into his arms.

"Dammit, darlin', I feel the same. I never thought this would happen to me, but it has. The moment I heard that biker creepin' through your house—that's when I realized just how much you mean to me. If that bastard had hurt you..."

As he placed his hands on either side of her face and stared down at her, a swell of emotion filled her heart.

"Clint, there's stuff you don't know," she stammered, trying to swallow back the heat in her throat.

"That goes both ways," he said solemnly, "but we know how we feel about each other, and that's what matters. We'll find our way through everything else."

"But, uh, I, uh, I lied to you."

"You think I don't know that?"

"What...?"

"You think I believed that story about gettin' lost on your way to Devlin's cabin? You can't ride past that huge rock without seein' it."

"Why didn't you say anything?"

"First, you're the cutest girl I've met in a long time and I didn't want to start off by makin' accusations. Second, I wanted to see how long it would take you to tell me, and third, I figured you must have needed to meet me real bad."

"I don't know what to say—but Clint, there's so much more..."

"Hey, I'm sure there is, and I'm dyin' to hear it, but this isn't the time or the place. Just know I'm crazy about you, and you're gonna get your butt spanked."

"What?"

"You heard me, oh, and one more thing. Devlin's comin' up for a visit. Matilda is busy bakin' until who knows when for a party she's caterin' and he wants to get out from under foot. He'll come by here to meet Gwen and Oreo, then head up the mountain."

"Does that mean Matilda's store is closed?"

"I guess it does," he replied thoughtfully. "That girl's a Whirlin' Dervish, but even she can't be in two places at once."

"But that means we won't be able to talk—unless we do it on the drive, and I'd rather be in front of the fire with a drink in my hand."

"Tiffany, relax. There's no rush."

"I guess I'm just anxious."

"Hey, I get it, keepin' secrets isn't easy," he said with a sigh. "I have a few of my own, believe me. Are you ready to head home?"

"I just need to grab Molly's plastic tub. Her supplements and grain are bagged up for a month. I think that's all I need."

"What about her blankets? You should probably bring a couple in case we have weather. There's still a chance of a late season storm."

"Good point," she exclaimed, stepping away to open a locker. "I just had them cleaned so they're folded and packed in plastic."

"I'll take them out to the Jeep and wait for you there," he offered, walking over and picking them up, "and Tiffany," he added, lowering his voice, "everything will work out."

As he shot her a wink and strode from the room, she let out a heavy, relieved sigh. What he'd said was almost too good to be true, and his parting words meant the world to her. But she wasn't convinced she was out of the woods, not yet. Gathering herself together, she walked across to a storage cabinet and lifted out the plastic container holding the baggies of supplements.

"Oreo's like a different horse," Gwen exclaimed, walking in and startling her. "Sorry, I didn't mean to scare you."

"It's not your fault, I was a million miles away. Did Clint mention I'll be staying with him for a little while."

"Yes, he told me. I'm really happy for you, and I'm so excited about Devlin Pike. I can't believe a famous daredevil rodeo star will be helping me with Oreo. I appreciate this more than I can say. Clint's a great guy."

"He is, and Gwen…I'm crazy about him."

"That's obvious," she said with a wink. "So—what are you going to do about it?"

"That's a very good question, and I don't have a good answer. Any advice?"

"Give it time, but you need to tell him who you are right away."

"I knew you'd say that. Does that include telling him about you?"

"That's a problem, but if you hold anything back he'll know, so you probably should, though you didn't hear that from me."

"I understand, and you're right, he'd sense it."

"He has sharp instincts just like I do. For example, I'm aware you've been wanting to change your life for a while now."

"Oh, my gosh."

"We'll talk about that another time. He'll be sitting in that Jeep tapping the steering wheel wondering what's taking you so long."

"Gwen, thanks for everything. You've been amazing. You *are* amazing. Please be careful."

"You know I will, and I'll let you know how things are going with Devlin. Wow, Devlin Pike. I still can't believe it."

* * *

Clint was in the Jeep, but he wasn't waiting impatiently.

The sheriff had called with unexpected news.

Their conversation had just come to an end when Clint saw Tiffany hurrying towards him.

"Sorry I took so long," she said breathlessly as she climbed in.

"It's okay, hon, I've been talkin' to the sheriff, and wait 'til you hear what he told me."

CHAPTER SIXTEEN

Driving away from the barn and heading towards the mountain, Clint told Tiffany the startling news.

Paul Darrow was Dirk Griswald's cousin, and Barney Parker was involved with both of them.

"Barney wasn't just coverin' up what Paul was doin' with the horses. That was the tip of the haystack. You know how vendors in motorhomes sell merchandise at the bigger shows?"

"Sure."

"Barney was supplyin' them with the stolen items from my stores, and other retailers as well. He took off the Kincaid labels and claimed it was excess inventory or stock from places goin' out of business."

"No! That snake!"

"He's hinted he might offer up the location of the storage facility in exchange for leniency."

"Are you okay with that?"

"Yes and no," Clint replied with a dark frown. "That man needs to spend some time behind bars, and that's what I told the sheriff. But I have no real say in it. All I can do is wait and see how it pans out."

"But Clint, there's one thing that's bothering me. Maybe I'm being paranoid—shit, there's that word again—

"What is it?" he asked, cutting her off.

"Dirk! After you slammed the door in his face and punched him, he said, *you'll both pay for this."*

"Tiffany, he'll be locked up. He *is* locked up."

"I know, but doesn't he have a gang?"

"The sheriff is already roundin' them up," Clint said solemnly as he started driving up the trail. "They'll be too busy findin' lawyers and stayin' outta prison to think about much else."

"I hope you're right, but it's hard not to worry."

"When we get back to the cabin I know exactly how to take your mind off all that," he remarked, lowering his voice and shooting her a look that sent butterflies fluttering in her stomach. "First, I'll spank your butt for lyin', then—"

"Hold on a second," she interrupted. "What about you?"

"What about me?"

"You said you knew from the outset I wasn't lost. You lied to me too."

"I didn't say one word about you bein' lost or not lost. I listened to your story and I took care of you."

She paused.

He had a point.

"I think that's called the sin of omission," she retorted. "Or is it a lie by omission? Something like that."

"I was also givin' you ample time to come clean...and you had plenty of opportunity, but you didn't."

"I just did."

"A little too late to save your butt, and as I was sayin', first I'll spank you, then we'll have a chat. You know all about me, but I know nothin' about you."

"All about you? Not really. I mean, I know who you are, but you could have a girlfriend, and I don't know anything about your family."

"Do you think for one minute—if I had a girlfriend—we would have been naked in your bed?"

He had a scolding tone to his voice, and she felt her face burn red.

"No, sorry, I shouldn't have said that."

"What kinda guys have you been datin'?"

"Not many," she said with a sigh. "Anyway, I am sorry. That just sort of, came out."

"I live in a house on the side of a mountain. I often have visitors, but they're usually related to my business. Have I entertained women up there? Sure, but there hasn't been anyone serious in my life for quite some time. I used to go clubbin' but I don't any more. There. Now it's your turn. I assume there's no man in your life, or is there?"

"No, just like you, I'm not like that," she shot back indignantly. "Naturally I've dated, but for the last year, not so much. I did have a boyfriend in college. I foolishly thought it would be forever, but for various reasons that didn't happen. It hurt a lot for a while, but now it feels like a lifetime ago and I'm glad we broke up. He wasn't into horses, and I'm passionate about them."

"Good, now that's done with, turn on the Aldean CD. That bastard Griswald exposed a gapin' hole in my security and I need to think about how to handle things goin' forward. I guess I should be grateful. Things could've been a lot worse."

* * *

Though Clint tried to focus on finding a solution, his mind kept drifting back to the beautiful young woman in the passenger seat next to him.

She had jolted his world far more than the thefts.

And she had evolved into a mystery.

From what he could gather, she hadn't been in Elk Valley for very long, and he found it curious she was boarding her mare at such a small barn.

The facility didn't have a name, and there was no trainer.

How had she even found it?

She'd been spending time at the show, which wasn't

unusual, but if she wasn't interested in having a trainer and competing, why and how did she know Paul Darrow?

But there was another question burning through Clint's brain.

How had she known the location of his mountain cabin?

It wasn't exactly on the beaten track, nor in a direct line from Devlin's place even if he had mentioned it.

As he glanced across at her, he couldn't deny his growing feelings, but he had a sneaking suspicion she was carrying a heavy secret—maybe more than one.

Continuing to drive carefully up the slope, he became resolved to get answers to all his questions. Every last one of them.

CHAPTER SEVENTEEN

Arriving at his mountain home and rolling to a stop, Clint saw Jethro march from the barn wearing a wide smile.

"Clint, that mare and Leroy are crazy about each other, and Buck likes her too," he exclaimed as he reached the Jeep. "He's been hangin' around her since you left."

"Molly is extremely friendly, and she loves dogs" Tiffany exclaimed, climbing out.

"She sure does, but Leroy—what a hoot! If Molly walks into the corral, Leroy follows her and they mess around over the fence. If she goes back inside, he follows her there too. He's really enjoyin' the company."

"Hey, Tiffany, why don't we take them for a ride?" Clint suggested. "There's a spot about thirty minutes further up I'd love to show you."

"That sounds great, and I'm sure Molly would enjoy stretching her legs. But I have to let her know I'm back, then freshen up," she said, grabbing her container of supplements.

"Go ahead. I need to talk to Jethro. I'll see you in a bit."

"Okay," she called, then hurried into the barn

"Jethro, I need to have a conference call with the store managers and the security team," Clint directed as they walked into the house. "The guy behind the robberies has been arrested, but I need to figure out how we can stop this happenin' in the future. Maybe the doors and windows need different locks and alarms."

"The security team should be able to come up with something," Jethro said confidently. "By the way, if you want the

Jeep up here I can take one of the ATV's back down."

"Yeah, that would be good. This is the first real emergency I've had, and it's made me realize I should keep a vehicle here permanently. Go into my office and get everyone on that call while I rustle us up some coffee. That's a lot to talk about."

* * *

After giving Molly some carrots and returning to the house, Tiffany decided on a long soak in a hot tub rather than a shower. Pouring in several dollops of foaming bath gel, she slid into the steaming water and closed her eyes. Thinking back to her time in bed with Clint, a delicious sensation rippled through her body.

First I'll spank you, then we'll have a chat. You know all about me, but I know nothin' about you.

As his threat flashed through her head, her eyes popped open. If she wanted to be with him she'd have to tell him everything.

All of it.

She didn't dare leave anything out.

But she didn't want to keep anything from him, and she was sure he'd understand.

Her resolve relaxed her, and she allowed herself the luxury of sinking into the hot, foamy water to doze.

* * *

"Tiffany…?"

Slowly opening her eyes, she found Clint leaning over her, then realized the bath was barely warm.

"I must have fallen asleep," she muttered with a yawn.

"Not surprisin'," he remarked, picking up a large, thick towel and holding it open for her. "Careful gettin' out. Do you still wanna go on that ride, or do you need to nap some more?"

"I'm fine now," she replied, climbing from the tub and resting against him while he wrapped it around her body. "I definitely want to take Molly out, but maybe have a quick bite to eat and cup of coffee first."

"Get dressed and I'll meet you in the kitchen."

"Okay, and Clint..." she murmured, gazing up at him, "there's stuff I need to tell you."

He smiled down at her, then turned and strode through the door

Quickly drying off and blow-drying the ends of her wet hair, she left the bathroom and found her bag waiting on the bed. Dressing in a clean pair of riding jeans, comfortable shirt, a warm sweater, and pulling on a pair of long socks, she slid her feet into her boots and hurried down the hall. Entering the kitchen she found Clint scrambling eggs and frying tomatoes, and a stack of buttered toast sat in the middle of the table.

"Wow, Clint, is there anything you can't do?" she exclaimed, pulling out a chair.

"Hold on, before you sit down," he said sternly, picking up a wooden spoon from the counter. "We have some unfinished business."

She knew what was coming.

A flurry of butterflies abruptly fluttered in her stomach.

"But, uh—"

"I'm a man of my word. Lower your pants to your thighs and lean forward."

"Clint..."

"Don't make me tell you a second time!"

Nervously sliding down the zipper and shimmying down the jeans, she rested her hands on the tabletop. Staring at him as he walked towards her, she felt her face flame red.

"Open your mouth and hold this between your teeth," he

ordered, presenting her with the spoon's handle. "You don't have to worry about Jethro, he left. Now arch your back," he continued as she bit down on the wood.

His hand roamed over her naked backside sending goosebumps popping across her skin, then the first hot slap landed, quickly followed by a second and third.

"No more lyin'," he scolded as he spanked, "not about anything. Lies never end well, and if we want to see where this thing goes the trust has to be there."

Abruptly taking the spoon from between her lips, he swiftly delivered several hard swats, making her yelp and throw her hands behind her.

"I'm sorry, you're right," she gasped, staring at him over her shoulder with wide eyes. "Please—I get it, I do."

"Hands down. Three more on each cheek, then we're done."

"But—"

"Do you wanna make it six?"

"No, no," she shot back, placing her palms back on the table.

"Let's see if you can do as you're told. Don't make a sound."

He lightly tapped the spoon in the center of her left cheek, landed it with a hard smack, moved it down an inch, tapped and smacked again, then finished with the same pattern on her sit spot. Though it had been almost impossible, she'd managed to stay silent.

"Good," he murmured. "Now the other side."

She grit her teeth as he delivered the stinging spoon, but when he finished he spun her around and held her tightly.

"This is who I am, darlin'," he whispered in her ear. "I'll tie you up, tease you, blindfold you, and yeah, I'll be spankin' you. Can you handle it? Are you sure you wanna be with a guy like me?"

CHAPTER EIGHTEEN

"God, yes," Tiffany replied breathlessly, melting into Clint's muscled arms. "I've been waiting for a man like you my whole life."

"Stay that again, but leave out—*a man like*."

Pulling back, she stared up at him.

"I've been waiting for you my whole life."

"Even though your ass is red and stingin'?"

"Uh-huh."

Abruptly leaning in, he pressed his lips on hers in a crushing kiss.

"Damn, girl..." he grunted as he pulled away. "I wanna take you back to my room and keep you there all day."

"That works for me."

"Nope, you're puttin" your sore ass in the saddle and we're goin' on that ride, but first you need to eat. Zip up those jeans and sit down."

Though she gingerly settled into the chair, when he placed the scrambled eggs and fried tomatoes in front of her, she realized just how hungry she was. As she began to devour the delicious meal, he poured hot coffee into their mugs, then sat opposite her.

"This is delicious," she exclaimed, "what did you—" but before she could finish Buck appeared through the doggy door and barked.

"He always knows when food's bein' served," Clint remarked with a chuckle, picking up a piece of toast and feeding it to him.

"He probably smelled it," Tiffany said, grinning as the dog

whined for more. "He's so cute, but I've been meaning to ask about his breeding. He's not like any dog I've ever seen."

"I think he's a mix between a German Shepherd and a Red Setter. He's as sweet as can be, but he's a talker, and real protective when he needs to be. I guess he's a bit spoiled, but that's okay. He deserves every last bit of it."

* * *

Looking across the table at Tiffany as she reached down to pet Buck, Clint's heart melted. He loved her sassy sense of humor, and the chemistry between them crackled. It seemed everything was finally coming right.

Dirk Griswald and his partners in crime had been arrested, and the sheriff seemed confident he'd find out where the stolen merchandise was being stored. But in spite of the good news, Clint knew Tiffany had a heavy confession—or confessions—to make.

"Would you like some more?" he asked, rising to his feet and picking up her empty plate.

"No, thanks, that was fantastic, and I'm looking forward to that ride."

"I am too. The view is indescribable. The first time I saw it I could hardly breathe. Talk about God's Majesty," he declared, carrying the dishes to the sink.

"Where can I find a cloth to wipe them?"

"I'm just rinsin' and droppin' them into the dishwasher," he replied. "You can go to the barn and get Molly ready."

"Are you sure I can't help?"

"I'm sure, and I need to change my boots. Speaking of changin', do you have a warm jacket you can ride in? The one I gave you probably won't be heavy enough for where we're goin'."

"Darn it, I don't. Sorry, I should have packed one."

"No problem, I have plenty," he said, loading the last plate in the dishwasher and closing it.

"Clint, hold on a second," she said softly, stepping up to him. "You asked me if I wanted to be with a man like you and I said, yes and I meant it, but I can't go on that ride until I talk to you. There's so much you don't know."

"Okay, ;et's go into the livin' room and get comfortable," he replied, placing an arm around her shoulders.

Hearing the words, *living room,* Buck, who had been watching them intently, ran to the hall, then stopped and barked.

"Wow, he's so smart," Tiffany exclaimed.

"Yep, and he's also impatient," Clint remarked with a grin. "Come on, I'm sure it's not as bad as you think."

But as he led her through to the cozy lounge and they sank into the comfortable couch, she appeared to be so anxious he prepared himself for just about anything.

"I'm not sure where to start," she muttered as a frown crinkled her brow.

"The beginnin' is usually a good place."

"I'm not sure where that is. Remember when we were with the sheriff and he said the FBI had sent an agent here?"

"Sure, they're after Griswald too."

"Well, uh, you're looking at her."

Clint's heart skipped, and for a moment he thought he'd misheard.

"This is my first real case," she continued. "They sent me because I know this place and the people here."

"I'm speechless," he muttered. "But if you're a trained field agent, why couldn't you tackle Dirk Griswald in your garage?"

"Yeah, I'm trained, and part of that training is knowing when to fight. I might have been able to defend myself for a short time, but I knew he'd get the better of me and I'd end up battered and bruised for no reason. Besides that, it was too soon."

"What do you mean, too soon?"

"Do you remember the murder of a guy called Jay Whittaker? He lived in a walled home above the lake."

"Sure, Matt, Callum and Devlin were involved in that. He was some kind of a crime boss, right?"

"Yes, he was. We know Dirk worked with him, but we're not sure how or why. When you said the sheriff told you Paul was Dirk's cousin, I already knew that. I was supposed to get close to Paul through the horses."

"So that's why you were sneaking around the trailer!" Clint exclaimed. "I'm surprised you didn't board your horse at Paul's barn."

"We discussed it, but, uh, they wanted me to stay close to my handler."

Clint stared at her, then shook his head.

"Not Gwen…surely not Gwen."

"Uh-huh. That ditzy persona is an act, though she genuinely needs help with Oreo. She's semi-retired, but they called her to support me."

"This is crazy. You're young and inexperienced. How could they put you in charge of a case like this?"

"Hey, I'm not in charge, I'm a minor player, but I'm in a position to be around Paul and Barney. Those guys wouldn't suspect me of working for the FBI, not for a second."

"So...ridin' up here and claimin' you were lost…did that have anything to do with all this?"

"Yes," she admitted, lowering her eyes. "I'm supposed to keep tabs on everything on your end, and, uh, protect you. I didn't know we'd end up..uh..together. I'm sorry I couldn't tell you. Actually, I shouldn't be telling you now."

CHAPTER NINETEEN

Clint didn't respond, not because he was angry, but because her story sounded absurd. It was hard to believe Tiffany was an FBI agent tasked with his safety, and spying on Paul, Barney, and a biker thug.

"Please say something," she mumbled, staring at him with pleading eyes. "If you're mad and want me to go, I'll understand, and again, I'm sorry. They don't even want the sheriff knowing my role yet. But the last, and perhaps the most important thing is —I've decided the job isn't for me. I thought it was, and I really enjoyed the training, but it's not what I want to do. I'm telling Gwen as soon as I can. I wanted to say something when we were there, but it was impossible."

"Tiffany, first of all, I'm not mad," he exclaimed. "Confused, yes, but not mad."

"Confused about what?"

"How could anyone put you in a position to go up against someone like Griswald. That's insane."

"Actually, it makes perfect sense. Like I said, Griswald would never suspect me."

"That's not the point."

"For my bosses, that was exactly the point."

"Besides Gwen, is there anyone else with you? A field agent who could actually tackle these guys?"

"They said someone unofficial would be watching over things, but they didn't tell me who."

"Small comfort," Clint muttered. "Regardless, we need to deal with this right away. Contact Gwen and let her know you're out."

"It doesn't work like that. At least, I don't think it does. I'm not sure, it's not like I've done this before."

"Tell her the truth. It's too much for you and you're in over your head. There's nothin' to be ashamed of. When I started out I wanted to be like Devlin."

"A stunt rider?"

"Yep, but I knew pretty quick it wasn't for me, and I stopped before I got hurt. This is similar. You got lucky with Dirk. You need to move on before that luck runs out."

"You're right," she said with a heavy sigh. "That's exactly how I feel. So…you're not mad at me?"

"No, darlin'," he said, softening his voice, "and I'm relieved you told me."

"You can't say anything. I'll get in all kinds of trouble. I'm just not cut out for all this cloak and dagger stuff. It's nothing like I thought it would be."

"That speaks well of you," he remarked with a grin. "We'll go for that ride, you can relax and gather your thoughts, and when we get back you can call Gwen."

"That sounds like a plan."

Moving his arms around her and hugging her tightly, he let out a heavy, grateful breath. Then suddenly wondered if Griswald had found out she was FBI, and that was why he'd returned to her house.

"Tiffany, you need to stay here until all this is cleared up," he said solemnly as he released her. "Just to be on the safe side."

"I was thinking the same thing. You don't mind?"

"Hmm, let me think…you naked in my bed every night, and ready to be ravaged when I wake up. No, I don't mind."

* * *

* * *

A short time later, Clint and Tiffany were tacked up and ready to head out. As they started off Buck ran ahead, then stopped and looked back at them.

"See? Impatient," Clint remarked with a chuckle. "He wants to run."

"Don't you have to worry about him getting attacked by the wildlife?" Tiffany asked. "Surely there must be wolves and other predators around."

"I've never had any problems, but that's why I carry this," he replied, touching the scabbard holding his rifle. "I haven't had to use it, but it's nice knowin' it's there, and he's trained not to leave my sight. That's why he stops and looks back."

"Have you ever seen any animals that concern you?"

"Not when I'm out ridin', but sittin' on the terrace I've caught glimpses. There are bears up here, and wolves, probably mountain lions too. But I'm careful with the garbage. I don't ever leave scraps around to entice them."

"It's so quiet and peaceful. I can understand why you love it up here, but it must be brutal in the winter."

"I don't stay here in the bad months. I stick around for the first snow, then I'm outta here. I lock up, ride Leroy down, and have a trailer waitin' at the bottom. I usually keep him at Lone Pine Ranch, but this year he might stay at Devlin's new place. Lone Pine Ranch has become so successful Callum probably won't have room. Devlin has already invited me."

"What about you? Where do you stay?"

"I have a lakeside cabin. Speakin' of places to live, that house you're in sure didn't feel like a home."

"It's where the FBI put me. I suspect it's sometimes used as a safe house, though it sure wasn't very safe for me. Mind you, I had to give my address to Barney. I was supposed to work at the show. I applied but he didn't have any openings. Uh, Clint, this trail is getting a bit steep."

"It's only for a short distance. Hold on—Buck, stay close, boy," he called. "Tiffany, I need to warn you," he continued as Buck ran back to him. "When we reach the top it appears to be a drop off. See how it looks like we're reachin' the edge of a cliff?"

"I sure do, and it's scary as hell."

"Is it makin' your stomach flip?"

"Hell, yeah," she exclaimed. "In fact, I want to stop and get off."

"I felt the same the first time I came here, and that's what I did. Go ahead. I'll wait."

"Please join me. I need to hold your hand."

"I'll be happy to," he said with a grin.

As they climbed off their horses, he wrapped his fingers around hers, and they started walking the short distance to the top of the incline.

"This is so creepy," she muttered as they neared.

"I know, just keep goin'. There! Look!" he declared, waving his arm. "How amazin' is this?"

CHAPTER TWENTY

Tiffany caught her breath—and held it.

A flat plateau reminiscent of Lone Pine Hill stretched out in front of her, and beyond, towering over her like nature's skyscrapers, snow-capped, craggy peaks reached into the heavens.

"It's...it's..." she stammered as he hugged her from behind.

"Yeah, I know. There aren't any words."

"It's what you said before, God's majesty. I feel so tiny."

"We are. Bein' up here puts things in perspective."

"I'm suddenly cold," she remarked with a shiver as a frosty breeze whistled around her.

"That's why you needed that heavier jacket."

"You're not kidding. Have you ever been to the far edge?"

"Yep, once, and I never want to go there again. It's a sheer drop, and I can't even guess how far down. Gives me the willies just thinkin' about it."

"We should have a picnic here one day."

"We could bring up the ATV. I wouldn't want to do it with the horses."

"Why not?"

"They'd have to be tied. I wouldn't want them grazin' on what they'd see as a field, and God Forbid they were spooked and got loose. There'd be no stoppin' them if they took off for a gallop. It's not like Lone Pine Hill where they can run down the other side."

"I see what you mean, and...there's something sort of ghostly about this place."

"You feel it too?"

"Totally. Shoot, speaking of ghosts, I forgot to tell you something," she said, turning to face him. "Have you ever heard of Willoughby?"

"The ghost town in the middle of nowhere? Sure, I've heard of it but I've never been there."

"It's possible that's where Griswald's gang hangs out. There have been reports of bikers in the area. That's another thing I'm supposed to be checking out, but it's too barren. I can't just drive up there."

"You not drivin" up anywhere," Clint declared, turning her around. "The sooner you let Gwen know you're out, the better. "

"You're right, except, thinking about it…"

"Damn, you're havin' second thoughts. I can see it in your eyes."

"Not about staying with the agency, but walking away from this assignment. I've never been a quitter. I'm sorry, but I need to see it through."

"I wish I didn't, but I understand. How did you end up in the FBI in the first place?"

"They recruited me out of college."

"No kiddin'?"

"I passed all the tests. You should see me shoot. I could compete if I wanted to."

"There's a range in Dayville County. We can take a drive out there and you can show me, but we should probably get back. Devlin will be arrivin' soon and I have work to do before he gets here."

"Thanks for bringing me to this amazing place," she murmured, but as she started to hug him, she felt a tug on the reins looped around her elbow. Looking over her shoulder, she saw Molly's ears were pricked and her eyes were wide. "Clint, did you hear anything?"

"Nope, but look at Buck. He sure did."

A short distance away, his dog was softly growling and staring into the trees.

"Let's get out of here," she said nervously.

"Works for me," he agreed as Leroy suddenly turned and stared in the same direction. "We'll hand walk the horses down the slope. Hopefully that will help to settle their nerves. You know that old adage."

"Which one?"

"When you're on the horse's back, they take care of you. When you're on the ground, you take care of them."

"No, I haven't heard that before."

They started off, but both Molly and Leroy began to snort and jog.

"Any idea what kind of animal would be making them behave this way?" she asked, tightening her hold on the reins. "Molly hardly ever spooks like this."

"It'll be a predator of some kind. Buck, stay close," he said sharply as his dog made a move towards the trees.

"I'm trained to stay calm, but I'm officially nervous," she muttered, then suddenly stopped. "Clint, I just saw something move by that tree. I'm sure I did."

* * *

Clint's mind raced.

His instincts were telling him they were being watched by human eyes, not a four-legged predator, but he didn't want to mention his suspicions to Tiffany. She was worried enough.

Hoping to catch a glimpse of what she'd seen, he continued to study the thick forest as they continued down the sleep slope. But the horses started to settle and Buck suddenly lost interest.

"I think we can get back on and ride now," Clint suggested as they reached the bottom.

"Thank goodness," Tiffany exclaimed. "That was so creepy. I wonder what it was, though there's a part of me that's glad we didn't find out."

Climbing into their saddles, they rode home without any further trouble, but the incident remained in the forefront of both their minds.

"Clint, I'm sure we were being watched," Tiffany remarked when they arrived at the barn and dismounted. "It was a person I saw, I just know it."

"I had that feelin' too, but whoever it was must have taken off or Buck would have kept growlin'. I don't know what to make of it," Clint said with a worried frown as they lifted the saddles off their horses.

"It's so unnerving," she muttered, then taking a breath, she added, "I just had a thought. How did he find this place? Oh no, hold Molly."

"Tiffany—what are you doin'?" he asked as she hastily handed him the reins and ran outside, but quickly stepping to the door he had his answer. She was on her back reaching beneath the Jeep.

"A tracker!" she exclaimed, rising to her feet and holding up a black box.

CHAPTER TWENTY-ONE

Quickly releasing the horses into their stalls, Clint hurried outside to join Tiffany and study the small black box in her hand.

"Are you sure that's what it is?" he asked as he neared.

"No question. It must have been planted when we were in town."

"Hey, Clint, hi, Tiffany! I see you found the tracker."

The deep male voice caught them by surprise, and spinning around they stared in disbelief as Matt ambled towards them.

"Matt! I thought you were outta town!" Clint exclaimed.

"I was. Now I'm back, and it was me followin' you down that slope. I'm sorry if I scared you."

"Why didn't you let us know it was you?" Tiffany demanded.

"And give your horses a heart attack? They were already freakin' out. Suddenly steppin' out from the bushes wouldn't have helped."

"I'm always glad to see you, but what are you doin' here? Why were you watchin' us?" Clint asked. "And you just said, *you found it*. You knew about this tracker?"

"Yep, Callum called and told me what's been goin' on. I know Dirk Griswald and what he's capable of and hightailed it back here. I wasn't in the trees watchin' you, I was keepin' my eyes peeled for anyone who might be followin' you—namely him!"

"So you were our invisible bodyguard," Tiffany said with a grin. "I like it."

"Only for the last hour. I hiked up from Devlin's cabin and got here just as you were ridin' off'. Griswald loves trackers so the first thing I did was check under the Jeep, and sure enough, there it was. That's why I was watchin' for him while you were enjoyin' yourselves. And Tiffany, you should put it back."

"Put it back?" she repeated, staring at him. "Why would I do that?"

"Because we want to lure him up here," Clint declared. "We'll beat him at his own game."

"You got it in one," Matt said with a chuckle. "Besides, he'll have this location pinpointed by now."

"Good grief. I know he's with the sheriff, but his gang could show up," Tiffany exclaimed.

"They won't without him," Matt assured her. "But let's go inside. I'll tell you what I know about Dirk Griswald and what we can do about him."

* * *

As Matt and Tiffany settled at the kitchen table, Clint brewed a fresh pot of coffee and set mugs out, along with a small pitcher of cream.

"How's Becky and the baby?" Tiffany asked. "Did they come back with you?"

"She's still with her parents. I don't want her around while Dirk is on the prowl. When this business is put to bed she'll come home."

"So—how do you know him?" Clint asked as he set the carafe of steaming coffee on the table.

"The Marine Corp."

"Dirk Griswald was a marine?" Tiffany exclaimed.

"For five minutes," he replied. "I suspect his family pushed him into the service hopin' it would straighten him out. It didn't. You don't wanna mess with him. He looks for trouble, and he'll fight at the blink of an eye just to show how mean he is. The guy is a real psycho."

"Clint got the better of him," Tiffany said proudly.

"How did you manage that?" Matt asked, staring at Clint. "Dirk never gives up."

"I had help from a door."

"I have to hear this story."

As Clint described the quick but effective battle with Dirk at Tiffany's home, Matt took a drink of his coffee, then set down his mug and shook his head.

"I don't know if that's good or bad," he remarked. "Dirk won't rest until he gets even. But that aside, what's your biggest issue in this whole mess with him?"

"I need to find out where he's hidin' the merchandise he stole from my stores," Clint exclaimed. "It seems he's sold some of it, but there's no way he could have moved it all. He must have it stashed."

"The sheriff thinks Paul Darrow will talk," Tiffany said hopefully. "We're just waiting to hear."

"I doubt that," Matt said solemnly. "He and Barney know Dirk will rip them apart if they do."

"Excuse me," Clint said, lifting his phone from his pocket as it chimed. "Ah, it's the sheriff. He must have some news. Hello, Sheriff. Tiffany's here, I'm going to put you on speaker. Okay, go ahead."

"I'm sorry to tell you this," the sheriff began solemnly, "but Paul Darrow and Barney Parker are refusin' to speak, and now they're bein' represented by Dirk Griswald's lawyer. In spite of what Tiffany overheard, we have no hard evidence any of them were involved with the burglaries, though we can connect Darrow to the horse dopin'. We found his syringes and drugs, but Dirk Griswald—I'm sorry he'll be released."

"But he attacked Tiffany in her garage," Clint exclaimed, "and what about the fight I had with him at her home? You arrested him. I don't understand."

“Unfortunately, Dirk is sayin’ he and Tiffany were seein’ each other and all that happened was a lover’s tiff. But I have officers out interviewin’ the neighbors. Hopefully someone witnessed something.”

“This is crazy! I wasn’t seeing Dirk Griswald,” Tiffany said angrily.

“The incident is still officially under investigation,” the sheriff continued. “I’m doin’ all I can, but if no-one saw him shove you—“

“But Sheriff, how can you let him go?” Clint demanded, cutting him off. “Dirk broke into Tiffany’s house. I had to defend her. You arrested him. Surely that’s cut and dried.”

“When there’s a slick lawyer involved, nothin’s cut and dried. There’s no question he went inside the house, but he claims Tiffany invited him over and left the front door unlocked so he could get in. You attacked him because you were jealous. He’s talkin’ about pressin’ charges.”

“What? This is insane.”

“Clint, you and I know that, but there’s no sign of a break-in. Tiffany, did you leave the front door unlocked? Is there another way into the house?”

“I never use the front door. I always go in and out through the garage.”

“So that’s a question mark,” the sheriff muttered. “I’m sorry, the prosecutor has already told me he doesn’t think there’s enough to go forward against Dirk. It looks like I’ll be releasing him.”

CHAPTER TWENTY-TWO

Ending the call, barely able to control his anger, Clint pushed back from the table and marched across the kitchen to stare out the window.

"This is so wrong," Tiffany groaned, dropping her head in her hands. "How can something like this happen?"

"It could be a blessin' in disguise," Matt suggested. "If he's out, he'll come up here to get even."

"Dammit, you're right," Clint said excitedly, spinning around, "and believe me, I'll get him talkin'."

"He's a careful sonofabitch. He won't exactly walk up and ring the doorbell," Matt remarked. "We need to talk about how to handle this."

"There's only one way in and that's on the track I cleared, and when he shows up, I'll be waitin'," Clint said vehemently.

"Are you sure?" Tiffany asked. "Can't he go around the rocks and trees?"

"He can try, but that's tough, and he'll find that out pretty quick. Not to mention the animals on the prowl."

"What if he shows up with his thugs?" Tiffany pressed. "Matt, you know him, would he do that?"

"It's possible, but he's more likely to come alone. It's a pride thing. He'll want to get his revenge without help from anyone, and he'll want to do it fast. He'll be a ragin' bull right now. Normally I'd say put up surveillance equipment, but he'll be expectin' that."

"Clint...I have an idea," Tiffany said thoughtfully. "Why don't you pretend to be gone. Lock up the Jeep, move the horses down to Devlin's, and have the house in darkness. Let him break in then—"

"Ambush him," Matt interjected. "That's not bad. Even if he thinks the place is empty he'll want to smash it to pieces and see what he can steal while he's here."

"Assuming he shows up," Tiffany mumbled.

"He'll show up," Matt declared. "He has to, and not just for his ego. He has to prove to his followers he's still the toughest guy on the block."

"Okay, so if we're here, who will be at Devlin's place with the horses and Buck?" Tiffany asked. "We can't leave them unattended."

"You, of course," Clint exclaimed. "Matt and I will handle the great hulk. But now that I think about it, I don't want you down there by yourself. I'll call Jethro. He can—"

"Babysit?" she retorted. "Did you forget I'm FBI?"

"You're FBI?" Matt said, staring at her. "I'm impressed. Tell me more."

"Excuse me," Clint interrupted, "Tiffany, I didn't forget, and nor did I forget what happened in your garage."

"You two can argue about that later. We need to stay focused," Matt said solemnly. "Are we agreed we'll arrange an ambush here?"

"Yes," Clint and Tiffany replied in unison, then smiling down at her, Clint added, "it's a great suggestion."

"I have them sometimes," she quipped, "and the conversation about me staying at Devlin's isn't over. But we need to call him and make sure this is okay."

"I'm sure it will be, and I'll leave you to sort out your differences," Matt declared. "I'm takin' off, but please, no bloodshed," he added with a grin.

* * *

* * *

Standing outside and watching Matt march away, Tiffany rested her head against Clint's shoulder. For a moment she thought he might be right and she should stay with the horse's at Devlin's cabin. The last few days had been a whirlwind filled with chaos, drama and danger, and in spite of her training she felt overwhelmed. As they turned around and started towards the house, Clint ordered Buck into the barn to watch over the horses.

"I don't understand," she remarked as they entered.

"If I'm goin' to be busy, he stays guard and lets me know if any wildlife poses a threat."

"Does that happen often? The wildlife posing a threat, I mean."

"It did in the past, not recently though," he replied, guiding her down a wide hallway. "There have been times he's barked and I've gone out and not seen anything, but I still fired my rifle. That scares them away."

"Clint, where are you taking me?"

"Here," he said with a grin as they approached the double doors at the end of the hall. Pushing them open, he ushered her into his expansive bedroom. "Welcome to my lair."

"This is amazing," she muttered, admiring the king-sized four-post bed and floor-to-ceiling windows offering unobstructed views of the forest. "I see the terrace, but how do you get there. There's no sliding glass door."

"Nope," he replied, walking with her over the thick rug sitting on the dark, hardwood floors. "You get to it through here." Opening a solid wooden door he guided her outside. "The patio wraps around. I often sit out here and read, or work on my laptop," he added, gesturing towards heavy wooden chairs with quilted cushions and a couple of tables.

"No wonder you spend so much time in this place. It's a slice of heaven, and it's so quiet. I bet it helps you think clearly."

"It sure does, and Tiffany, I'm real clear about you."

"Me?" she said, her heart skipping as she gazed up at him.

"I don't know why, it's not something I can explain, but you're special, real special, and those aren't just words."

"Clint..."

"I feel bad you got caught up in all the craziness."

"It wasn't your fault. I'm the one who saw Paul Darrow inject that horse and overheard the conversation between Barney and Dirk."

"Yep, you sure did, but Paul is insignificant. Dirk's the issue, he always has been, and his involvement with my business has put you in danger, real danger. It's my job to make sure nothin' else happens to you."

"Oh, I see," she replied, tilting her head to the side. "That's why you're insisting I stay at Devlin's while you two are up here."

"You got it," he replied firmly, moving her back inside, "and I'm about to make sure that's exactly what you'll do."

CHAPTER TWENTY-THREE

Before Tiffany could respond, Clint had her bent over the bed and spanking her through her jeans. But it wasn't having the desired affect. She was laughing between yelps.

"Stop," she squealed, looking at him over her shoulder with a wide grin.

"I'll stop when you promise not to give me any more lip about stayin' at Devlin's cabin…and what's so damn funny?"

"I don't know," she replied, then gasped as he landed an extra hard slap. "Please, just stop."

"Do you promise?"

"Yes, okay, I won't give you any more trouble."

"You're sayin' that like you don't mean it," he said warily.

"I do mean it," she insisted, hastily rolling onto her back and extending her arms. "Kiss me to seal the deal."

Placing his hands on his hips, he grinned down at her and shook his head.

"You, Tiffany Sullivan…" then without finishing his thought, he quickly undressed her.

"It's cold," she muttered, hastily climbing under the covers as he stripped.

"Oh, yeah? I can heat your ass up some more, and I wanna know what was so funny."

"Honestly, I'm not even sure myself," she replied, snuggling against him.

"Like I said, you're special, and I don't want you anywhere near that savage. Matt and I can handle him. We don't need your help."

"Probably not," she purred, wrapping her fingers around his stiffening cock, "but I'd still love to be here when you take him down."

"You can be here when the sheriff rolls up and arrests him again," Clint said huskily, "and if you keep strokin' me like that I'll have to do somethin' about it."

"I wish you would," she whispered, raising her head and planting soft quick kisses over his face.

"I'm thinkin'—"

"Don't think," she whispered, moving her lips to his ear.

"I'm thinkin'," he repeated forcefully, "you're just tryin' to get out of havin' your ass spanked some more."

"Maybe, but that doesn't mean I don't want this," she crooned, moving her fingers from his hardness to gently squeeze his balls.

Suddenly reaching down, he grabbed her hand, pulled it away, then rolled her onto her back and rested his weight on top of her.

"Ooh, you're crushing me," she moaned, squirming as he pinned her wrists on either side of her head.

"Darlin', you can't kid a kidder."

Suddenly pressing his lips on hers, he devoured her mouth in a crushing kiss until she stopped writhing beneath him.

"I knew you'd be a quick learner," he muttered, raising his head and staring down at her.

"Clint…you turn me on so much."

Abruptly sliding off her body and stretching out next to her, he thrust his hand between her legs.

"So it seems," he grunted, shoving a finger inside her, then dove his head to her breasts and sucked in her nipples.

Moaning loudly, she raised her chest to meet his mouth, but suddenly straightening up, he effortlessly rolled her over, pushed her legs apart and kneeled between them.

"Your butt's not near red enough," he muttered, slapping his hand from cheek to cheek. "You're goin' to Devlin's and that's that, are we clear."

"Yes, I'll go," she yelled urgently.

"I love your sassy mouth and your spirit, but you're still gonna end up with a scarlet backside."

Though she wanted to protest, it was only because she thought she should. She secretly loved the fiery kisses of his hard hand.

"Nothin' to say?" he demanded. "Don't tell me it only takes a few stingin' smacks to quiet that smart mouth of yours."

"You call them stinging?" she blurted out, then immediately wanted to take it back.

"Damn girl, you really like to push it," he exclaimed, quickening the speed and force of his flattened palm. "Does this sting enough for you?"

"Yes, yes, I was only kidding," she squealed. "Please, no more. I'm sorry."

"Are you sure about that?" he asked, stopping and pushing his fingers into her glistening sex.

"Oooh, Clint...yes, I swear."

"No more sass tonight?"

"No, I swear, none."

* * *

Leaning over Tiffany's body and reaching into the nightstand drawer, Clint retrieved a condom, swiftly tore open the package and sheathed his rigid rod. Placing himself at her entrance and hearing her catch her breath, he waited a moment, teasing her.

"Please, Clint...I want you so bad..."

As her heartfelt plea sent the blood rushing through his loins, he thrust into her warmth, then grabbed her hips and pumped with quick, strong strokes. Gazing down at her red cheeks and listening to her loud groans, he knew he wouldn't last long if he didn't slow down. Easing off, he reached under her body to search out her clit.

"Clint I love this so much," she purred, then gasped as he found her magic button and began to rub.

"Does this feel good too," he whispered, bending over her and pressing his lips against her ear. "I could stay buried inside you and tease like this and keep you right on the edge for a very long time."

"Ooh, no, please don't, I couldn't stand it."

"Just remember, I don't have to spank you to make a point. Do we understand each other?"

"Yes, yes," she panted as he rubbed harder. "Ooh, if you don't stop doing that I'll explode."

"Do you want to explode?"

"Yes," she whimpered, "but seriously…I'm getting…really…really…"

"You're gonna come right now, then come again with my cock," he growled, suddenly lowering his voice. "Do it! Do it now!"

As her body stiffened, he increased the pressure, then closed his eyes, savoring her cries and the feel of her pussy walls throbbing against him. When the last spasm petered out, she dropped on her elbows and rested her head against a pillow.

"You're not done yet, Princess," he muttered as he straightened up.

Taking his time, he languidly stroked, lightly spanking her upturned ass as the spirit moved him. As the minutes ticked by, she raised herself back up on her hands, and he reached beneath her to tweak her nipples. She yelped, then suddenly arched her back.

"Please, Clint, will you fuck me harder?"

Her voice had changed.

It was softer.

He smiled.

She had surrendered…

“Since you asked so nicely.”

Tightly grasping her waist, he changed his angle, pitched forward, and quickened his pace.

As he accelerated, she moaned loudly, and moments later, arched her back. Determined not to stop until she exploded a second time, he began vigorously pounding her pussy. But his moment was looming. He was about to slow down when she let out a cry.

“Please don’t stop. Please…?”

Her timing could not have been more perfect, and he continued to plunge in and out of her hot, wet channel until she was wailing her euphoria. It sent him over the edge, and with a guttural groan, he released in a dizzying, mind numbing eruption…

CHAPTER TWENTY-FOUR

Clint and Tiffany were still dozing when the ringing of his phone echoed through the room. Grunting, he rolled over, lifted his jeans off the floor and his phone from the pocket. Glancing at the screen he saw it was Matt.

"Hey, Matt," he muttered as he laid back and Tiffany snuggled against him. "What's up?"

"I just spoke with Devlin. Callum already told him about Paul Darrow druggin' the horses. Apparently one of them was Goliath, Kelly's horse."

"No! Dammit!" Clint growled. "Is he okay?"

"Yep, fine. Thanks to Tiffany they knew why he was actin' funny, and the vet was already there."

"Let me call you right back on my sat phone. This mobile only has one bar."

"Sure thing."

"Clint, what is it?" Tiffany asked as he ended the call.

"Paul drugged Goliath, Kelly's horse. He's okay, but I was about to lose the cell signal. I have to get back to Matt on the other phone."

"I'm coming with you," she exclaimed, hastily climbing from the bed, "except I think I'll stop by the kitchen. I'm dying for a cup of tea."

"Can you brew me up some coffee while you're at it?"

"For you, anything," she replied with a grin as they dressed.

As Tiffany headed off to make their hot drinks, Clint strode into his office and picked up the satellite phone.

"Hey, Matt, sorry about that," he said as Matt answered. "You were sayin' Paul drugged Kelly's horse."

"No problem, and yeah, he did. But the sheriff contacted the show committee and the classes have been put on hold while they're checkin' things out. It's a huge scandal. Paul's trainin' days are over, at least here in Elk Valley. Devlin was furious, and when I told him what happened with Tiffany he couldn't wait to get up to the cabin. As he put it, he wants to be a part of the *Get Griswald Posse!*"

"What about Callum?"

"He'd love to join us, but several of his clients are still showin' so he can't get away. Anyway, the barn here had some unused beddin' so I've put that in the stalls, but there won't be enough hay here for all the horses."

"I'll bring down a couple of bales in the jeep. When is Devlin plannin' on joining' us?"

"He's leavin' now. He'll be haulin' Merlin up as far as he can in his single horse trailer, then ridin' the rest of the way. He's pretty sure he can get here before sundown."

"Most of the snow is gone, he shouldn't have any trouble. There's plenty of room here if you wanna come back up, or you can stay with him. The sheriff said Griswald will be out in the mornin' so there's no rush."

"I'll give you and Tiffany some space," Matt replied with a chuckle. "We'll join you for breakfast, but we'll call before comin' up, then we can bring your horses down."

"Sounds like a plan. I'll see you shortly with the hay."

Ending the call, Clint grinned. The *Get Griswald Posse,* was the perfect description of the small group and the task ahead. Leaving his office, he headed to the kitchen to join Tiffany.

"I was just about to bring in your coffee," she declared, handing him a mug. "What's going on?"

"You're a star."

"I am? Why?"

"You told the sheriff about Paul injectin' the horses and he put out the alert, so Callum and Kelly knew why Goliath wasn't right. The vet arrived and took care of him and some others. Everyone owes you a huge debt of gratitude."

"I don't know what to say, except, I hope this means you're not mad at me anymore."

"Heck no, and you'll find out I never stay mad for very long," he replied with a grin. "I have to get some hay to Devlin's. He's bringin' Merlin up so I'm takin' three bales. But I'll drink this first and have a bite to eat. I'm a tad hungry, though I can't imagine why," he added with a wink.

"Funny thing, I am too," she quipped. "I'll grab some of those muffins I saw in the freezer and zap them."

"Sounds good."

"While you're gone I'll spend some time with Molly."

"I'm not leavin' you here alone."

"Why not?"

"Have you forgotten Griswald put a tracker on the Jeep? He knows where we are. You're comin' with me."

"What about Molly and Leroy?"

"I'll close the door that leads out to the corral and leave them plenty of hay. They'll be fine. We'll only be gone a short time. An hour at the most. And I'll leave Buck in the barn with them."

"I guess that will work, though I do feel weird leaving."

"When Molly's in her stall overnight at Gwen's there's no-one wandering around the barn."

"Uh, no."

"So what's the difference?"

"I see your point. Okay. But I still don't want to be at Matt's longer than we have to."

* * *

* * *

Dirk Griswald's lawyer, Joseph Arnold, had amassed a small fortune. His client was always in trouble, and Joseph was adept at prying him out of it. Now Dirk was facing a litany of charges, and once again, Joseph had woven an intricate word tapestry pointing out loopholes.

But while he had convinced the prosector the case would be an embarrassment, and could even end up being seen as a waste of the court's time, the sheriff was insisting he could keep Dirk behind bars until the following morning.

"We're still investigatin'," the sheriff exclaimed.

"Then be my guest, investigate," Joseph replied calmly. "You simply cannot keep my client locked up while you do it."

"The hell I can't. He's a menace. Didn't you read the charges? Two counts of assault, breakin' and enterin', conspiracy—"

"Stop right there, Sheriff," Joseph declared, holding up his hand. "Those so-called charges are simply the angry accusations of a woman scorned. My client is constantly harassed by the law, and we're both running out of patience. If you don't release him immediately, I will be filing an harassment suit against you and your department. It's entirely up to you."

CHAPTER TWENTY-FIVE

You don't have to like your clients to represent them.

Walking with Dirk out to the car, Joseph heard the words echo through his head. The day he'd passed the bar his father had offered the advice.

"It's not easy, but if you want to make decent money you'll learn how to do it."

His father had been right.

Joseph had never liked Dirk.

Other than promptly paying his bills, the muscled, tattooed biker had no redeeming qualities.

Many times Joseph had wanted to walk away.

But now he drove a new Mercedes, and lived in a lovely home overlooking the lake...all thanks to Dirk's habitual trouble with the law.

"Drop me behind Mike's garage then go straight home," Dirk grunted as Joseph drove from the parking lot. "If anyone asks, we spent the rest of the afternoon and into the evening together. You'll get a bonus at the end of the month."

"Please don't go after that girl," Joseph said solemnly. "There are only so many Get Out Of Jail Free cards."

"Hey, I'm not an idiot. There's a reason I'm still in business."

"You mean, besides the fact that I keep your ass out of the slammer?"

"Yeah, besides that! Joe, you should know by now I know how to push the envelope without tearing it. But if someone doesn't get the message the first time, I have to deliver it another way a second time and make sure it sticks. I don't like doin' it the third time. It's never pretty."

"Don't tell me anything more."

"I don't intend to. Just remember, if you get a call, whoever it is, say you can't talk because I'm with you."

"Yep, I know. I've been down this road a few times before," Joseph muttered as he turned down an alley.

"Stop next to that Toyota 4Runner."

"That thing's a beast," Joseph remarked, staring at the heavy- duty vehicle. "Where the hell are you going? Never mind. I don't want to know."

Wordlessly shooting Joseph a look, Dirk climbed out and slammed the door shut.

As Joseph turned his Mercedes around, he watched Dirk in the rear view mirror. The tough biker was lifting a key fob hidden on the top of the front left wheel. Accelerating down the street, a worried frown crossed Joseph's brow.

He had a bad feeling.

A *very* bad feeling.

* * *

Sitting behind the wheel of the SUV, Dirk opened the glove box, retrieved a phone and turned it on. As a map appeared on the screen with a blinking red light, a sneer curled his upper lip.

"Clint Kincaid," he growled. "You and that nosey bitch won't get away this time."

After securing it into a holder attached to the dashboard, he raised the center console. Inside was a revolver and a switchblade. Lifting out the gun, he checked the chamber, nodding his approval when he found it loaded. Placing it back in the compartment, he reached in front of the passenger seat and picked up a small, square bag. Sliding back the zipper and lifting the lid, he found a large bottle of water, a thermos, sandwiches in a Tupperware box, two packages of cookies and some energy bars. Satisfied, he zipped it back up and sat it on the seat next to him, then swiveling around, he peered into the back. A short goose down parka, a long, heavy coat and a blanket were waiting if needed.

When Joseph had initially visited him at the sheriff's office, Dirk had slipped him a note.

"Take it to Tom," he'd ordered. "He'll be at his Harley repair shop."

Tom Crenshaw was Dirk's right-hand man, and the message had been written in code.

Looking around and making sure there was no-one in sight, Dirk started up the powerful engine and rolled slowly down the alley. Reaching the end, he signaled, then turned left.

He'd obey every traffic law.

He couldn't risk getting stopped.

The SUV was stolen and had fake plates, but they were splattered with mud, though a deputy would soon clean them off if he needed to run them through the system.

* * *

Dirk had known about Clint's mountain hideaway for a while, and he'd made it a point to find out the exact location. The millionaire cowboy would have all sorts of treasures, and Dirk planned to pay the cabin a visit. He'd never imagined he'd end up going there to deal with a young woman who had put her nose where it didn't belong, and dealing with Clint Kincaid personally.

Though he knew the sheriff would have called Clint and warned him, Dirk wasn't worried. The cowboy probably thought he and the girl were safely tucked away on the side of the mountain. Even if he was worried, he'd expect any unwanted visitors to arrive in the middle of the night, not during daylight hours.

Dirk's only concern was the unfamiliar territory.

He always made it a point to survey his targets, know the best ways in and out, security systems and any obstacles he'd have to avoid or overcome.

A chill pricked his skin.

Rarely did he second-guess his decisions, but driving down the country road that would take him to the foot of the mountain, he wondered if he was making a mistake.

"No!" he snarled. "I never walk away!"

He glanced at this watch.

The thought of navigating back down at night held no appeal. But barring any unforeseen hiccups he'd be there well before sunset. Telling himself he'd make quick work of things, and he'd steal only the best pieces, not clean out Clint's entire house, he continued on with a steely determination.

CHAPTER TWENTY-SIX

Lead-footing it up the slope, Dirk wasn't thinking about the possibility of animals crossing his path, hitting a deep mud hole, or suddenly being faced with a downed tree limb. All he cared about was reaching Clint's cabin and taking care of him and the girl before sunset.

As a teenager he'd spent hours with his friends driving trucks through muddy terrain and up and down banks. He could handle the 4Runner. What he couldn't handle was the thought of coming back down the mountain in darkness.

When he was a young boy he'd been on a camping trip with a group of other children and their parents. Sitting around the fire he'd heard terrifying stories about horrifying creatures that lived deep in the mountain forest. Like vampires, they'd emerge at night to terrorize their victims in unimaginable ways.

Bizarre, petrifying images had haunted his dreams for years.

As he grew up he knew the tales were nothing but nonsense, but he still hated being in the woods—any woods—after dark. Every rustle of the leaves and whisper of the wind would cause his heart to race and goosebumps would break out on his skin.

Slowing down to take a sharp turn, he glanced at the red dot on the hi-tech gadgetry and let out a relieved breath. Clint's cabin was only thirty-minutes away. But as he raised his eyes, a short distance ahead and to the left was a huge, oddly shaped rock, unlike anything he'd seen.

As he drew closer, he began to wonder if it was a meteorite. The base was buried as if it had been slammed into the ground, and there didn't appear to be any other similar rocks nearby. Telling himself he'd have to come back one day to look at it more closely, he was about to accelerate when the red dot on the screen in front of him began to move.

He caught is breath.

It was headed in his direction.

Clint was on his way down the slope, and probably had the nosey, annoying girl with him. Being outdoors surrounded by forest was the last place Dirk wanted to meet them.

"Dammit to hell," he grunted, frantically looking around for somewhere he could park out of sight.

Suddenly spotting where the rough, makeshift road forked off in front of the mysterious rock, he quickly drove towards it.

And his mind began to race...

He could continue up to Clint's cabin and load the 4Runner with everything he could lay his hands on, then wait in the comfort of the mountain home for Clint and the girl to return. It was ideal...but they probably wouldn't get back until dark.

The red dot drew closer.

The first thing to do was get out of sight.

Pushing the thoughts from his mind and hastily backing up the SUV, he parked alongside the boulder, confident he'd be hidden as Clint drove down the slope.

* * *

After loading the hay into the Jeep, securing the stall doors leading out to the corrals, and settling Buck with a rawhide, Clint had walked into the house to get Tiffany. But he found her holding the satellite phone, wide-eyed and looking deeply worried.

"It's the sheriff," she declared, handing it to him. "You need to talk to him."

"Hey, Sheriff, is something wrong?" he asked feeling his pulse tick up.

"Hello, Clint, I'm not sure. One of my deputies just called and said he thought he saw Dirk Griswald drivin' a 4Runner up the mountain."

"When? Was your deputy sure it was him?"

"It was a little while ago, and no, he couldn't be sure. He and some buddies were hikin'. He would've called sooner but there was no cell service where they were. He tried to see the plates, but they were too far away and splattered with dirt."

"So, uh, what do you think?"

"I'm sendin' a squad car to patrol around the base. If it is Dirk, he'll have to come down, and if he was up to no good we'll be there. I understand that's no great comfort, but it's the best I can do. I wish I could send up one of my emergency vehicles, but I don't have enough information to do that. If I knew it was Dirk for sure, I would, but I don't, so..."

"Is there any record of him owning a Toyota 4Runner?"

"Nope, nothin' registered, not to him or any members of his gang. I ran them all."

"Thanks, Sheriff, I guess that's something. I'm about to take some hay down to Devlin's. I'll be sure to keep my eyes peeled."

"Clint, if you see him don't take the law into your own hands. Call me right away."

"I will if I can, but you know cell service is spotty up here."

"Take your sat phone with you."

"Oh, right, sorry, I blanked on that for a second. Yes, I'll be sure to do that."

But as he'd ended the call, Tiffany had grabbed his arm.

"Clint, we can't leave the horses. You know what a monster that man is. We just can't."

"I agree," Clint replied with a heavy breath.

"What do we do?"

“I’m callin’ Matt. He’s the expert when it comes to things like this.”

As Clint had hoped, Matt had the solution.

He would drive Devlin’s ATV up through the forest to Clint’s home. Once a Special Forces Commando, Matt had no concerns about tackling Dirk Griswald if he dared to show his face.

Now at the fork that led to Devlin’s cabin, Clint slowed down and made the turn, but as they passed the huge rock Tiffany suddenly grabbed his arm.

“Clint—” she stammered, her heart racing, “we just passed a 4Runner. It’s parked alongside the boulder.”

CHAPTER TWENTY-SEVEN

Glancing up at his rearview mirror, Clint could see the vehicle but not the driver.

"What do we do?" Tiffany asked breathlessly. "It has to be him."

"It could be someone enjoyin' the view, or they stopped to get a closer look at the rock."

"We have to find out," she exclaimed, swiveling in her seat and looking behind them. "Shit, it's leaving. It's pulling out and leaving."

"Is it goin' back down, or headed up towards my place?"

"He's going up! Do you think it's him?"

"I'm not takin' any chances. Call Matt."

"Already doing it," she replied, snatching the phone from the glove compartment. "I hope he has cell service."

"Hello, Clint, is that you?" Matt asked as he answered the call.

"Hi, Matt, it's me, Tiffany. We think we just saw Dirk Griswald heading up to the house. We couldn't see the driver, but it's a 4Runner."

"I'll be ready. Let Devlin know as well. If Griswald shows up I'll let you know right away."

"Okay," she replied, then quickly put in a call to Devlin and gave him the news.

"I know Matt can deal with just about anything," Devlin remarked, "but he should still have back up. I'll ride Merlin up through the forest. If it is Dirk in that 4Runner I'll beat him there."

"Great, thanks, Devlin. Please be careful, and I'll call Matt and let him know you're on the way."

"With those two meetin' him, maybe I'll finally find out where he has my stuff stashed," Clint muttered as Tiffany called Matt and gave him the heads up.

"We should go back too," Tiffany said urgently as she finished speaking with Matt.

"As I've said before, I don't want you anywhere near that bastard."

"But with Matt and Devlin there he won't stand a chance. Don't you want to interrogate him yourself?"

"Dammit," he grunted, hitting the brakes. "I want to go up, of course I do, but I don't want you there, and I don't want to leave you at Devlin's by yourself."

"Clint, I'm not going to lie, and you won't want to hear this, but if you drop me at Devlin's I won't be able to just sit there and twiddle my thumbs waiting for news. You know that."

"Dammit!" he repeated as he began to turn the Jeep around. "When we get there, you'll do *exactly* what I say. Got it?"

"Yes, sure, totally."

"Now call the sheriff. Let him know what's goin' on."

"Uh, Clint..." she said thoughtfully, "I just had an idea."

"I thought you just said you'll do as I say," he retorted sternly, his tires kicking up dirt as he sped forward.

"I'll call him, I will, just listen for a second. You want to know where Dirk's hiding your merchandise, but let's get real. It's highly doubtful he'll tell you. If you start beating him up he'll have bruises, and he has that slick lawyer. You and Matt and Devlin could end up being the ones in trouble, not Dirk. It almost happened once."

"I hate to say it, but you're right."

"And we already know he won't tell the sheriff anything."

"We sure do. What's your point?"

"I think I know how to get him talking without touching a hair on his head."

* * *

After throwing his lariat over his shoulder and diagonally across his body, Devlin looped a rope around Merlin's neck, jumped on his back, and started up the slope towards Clint's home. He'd be traveling as the crow flies, and he could already see plenty of clear space ahead. As he moved Merlin into a canter, the horse playfully tossed his head, then picked up the pace and leapt over a log. Devlin grinned. His horse was loving every minute.

The trip up the incline was quick and effortless for the big gelding, making Devlin feel more like a passenger than a jockey. But as they stopped in the shadows opposite Clint's mountain retreat, Merlin's ears pricked up. Seconds later, Devlin heard an approaching vehicle.

The 4Runner sped past, startling the horse, but he quickly settled, and as the SUV came to a stop, Devlin watched the brawny, leather clad biker step out. Devlin was sure Matt would have heard the vehicle, and would be waiting inside ready to tackle the thug. But Buck began to bark, and the brawny brute walked past the house and stood staring at the barn.

Devlin caught his breath.

The opportunity was too good to pass up.

The man was a stationary target with his back to him.

Lifting his lariat over his head, Devlin moved Merlin slowly forward.

The horse's footfalls were silent in the soft dirt.

Raising the rope, Devlin twirled it in the air…then let it fly.

The moment the lasso landed around Dirk's body, Devlin pulled it tight, then yanked him backwards onto the ground. Suddenly bursting through the front door, Matt raced across to the screaming biker, holding him down as Devlin jumped off Merlin.

* * *

As Clint and Tiffany drove up to the house, they were relieved to find Dirk Griswald laced in rope and sitting on the ground, with Buck a few feet away growling at him. Matt and Devlin, standing on the porch drinking a beer, turned and raised their cans.

"Howdy," Devlin called.

"What a wonderful sight," Tiffany exclaimed as she climbed from the Jeep. "Where's Merlin?"

"Happily enjoyin' some hay in the barn," Devlin replied with a grin. "Too bad you weren't here to join the party,"

"I wish I had been," Clint said, marching over to stare down at the prisoner. "Two questions, Griswald. How did you get into Tiffany's house, and where are you storin' all the stuff you stole from my stores?"

"Fuck you, asshole."

"Let me put it another way," Clint continued, leaning over him and lowering his voice. "You can tell me now, or tell me in far less comfortable circumstances."

"Oh, wow, I'm really scared," Dirk grunted with a sneer.

"Tiffany, while I go into the barn and get the ATV, why don't you take Matt and Devlin inside and tell them our plans. But make it quick. It'll be dark soon. "

"Nothing would give me greater pleasure," she replied, then catching Dirk's eye, she added, "See you soon."

CHAPTER TWENTY-EIGHT

When Clint had said, *But make it quick, it'll be dark soon,* he had been glaring down at Dirk, and noticed what appeared to be a flicker of alarm in the biker's steely eyes.

"What's the matter? You had no problem breakin' into my stores in the middle of the night."

"I don't know what you're talking about," Dirk grunted with a scowl, "and you can't keep me tied up like this. I haven't broken any laws. All I did was drive up here. This is fucking kidnapping. Let me go right now or I'll make sure my lawyer will take every penny you have, asshole."

"This particular piece of land is privately owned—by me—and you're trespassin', but it doesn't matter. There are no witnesses, just like there were none when you assaulted Tiffany. Your smart lawyer twisted that situation into a pretzel. This could be the same, but it will never happen."

"Oh, yeah, and why is that?"

"This story may never be told."

"I'll tell the fucking world about this bullshit."

"You won't be sayin' another word to anyone unless you tell me where you're hidin' my merchandise. If you don't, you'll meet a very ugly end."

"You wouldn't fuckin' dare," Dirk sneered. "You're one of the good guys. You don't have it in you. Me? I'm a bad guy. I can do shit like that."

"You're missin' something," Clint remarked, lowering his voice and crouching next to him. "Yeah, there are good guys and there are bad guys, but there are also cowboys, and that's what

I am. Matt and Devlin are too."

"What does that—?"

"Okay, Clint, let's do it," Devlin exclaimed, stepping out the front door and cutting off Dirk before he could finish.

Striding quickly across to the barn, Clint checked on the horses, then rolled out the ATV and called Buck to join him.

"Okay, Dirk, it's time to go for a ride," Devlin exclaimed as Matt and Tiffany left the house and joined him.

"I'm not goin' anywhere!"

"We're loadin' you into the ATV," Matt continued. "Put up a fight, no problem. We'll just drag you along the ground behind it. Your choice?"

"Fuck this shit!" Dirk screamed, but startled by the outburst, Buck bounded up to him, barking and snarling.

"Are you gonna play ball," Matt asked, raising his voice to be heard over the big, angry dog, "or should we let Buck convince you?"

"No, no, call him off!"

"Buck, come with me," Clint yelled.

As Buck ran over to the ATV, Matt and Devlin lifted Dirk, plopped him down on the passenger seat, and tightly tied him in. As Devlin settled in behind the wheel, Clint and Tiffany climbed in the back.

"Matt, don't you want to sit with us?" Tiffany asked.

"I'll be joggin' along with Buck. I like the exercise."

"Where are you takin' me?" Dirk asked, though his voice didn't carry its usual bluster.

"To a place that will help you think clearly," Devlin replied, "and if it doesn't, you won't be thinkin' about much of anything until you wake up in hell wishin' you'd done things differently."

* * *

* * *

As the ATV headed up the gentle slope, Clint stole glances at the evil man in front of him. He could see Dirk's bravado slipping away and fear creeping in. But the light was fading fast. They were running out of time. Finally the incline became steep, and moments later they were approaching what appeared to be the edge of a cliff.

"Where are we? What are we doing here?" Dirk yelled frantically as Devlin came to an abrupt stop.

"That depends on you," Clint replied, climbing off the back. "Matt, do me a favor and keep Buck next to you. I don't want him runnin' up to the edge and fallin' off."

"Sure thing. There's some extra rope here, I'll put it on his collar."

"Thanks, I should've thought to bring his leash."

"Fuck the dog," Dirk yelled. "What's—"

"Hey, shut up and listen," Clint barked, marching up beside him. "The sun's almost down but you can still see the end of the line. This is real simple. Either tell me what I want to know, or I'll put this ATV in drive, then step back. We'll all watch you go flyin' over the edge. And trust me, it's a long, long, way down."

"You can't, you'll be found out. They'll trace—"

"The ATV? Not a chance. The drop is forever. it will take you a week to hit the bottom."

"Clint, that's an exaggeration," Devlin piped up. "More like two days."

"You might be right," Clint replied with a chuckle. "Regardless, I doubt any human has ever set foot down there, and possibly never will. It looks almost prehistoric. It's a deep, narrow chasm. So, where's my stuff, Griswald?"

"I don't believe you. If I go over that edge, you'll never find it, and I told my lawyer I was coming up here. If I disappear, this is where everyone will come looking. Don't forget, the sheriff knows you have a problem with me. They'll find my car tracks, someone will have seen me. Nah. You're not that stupid...or maybe you are. Maybe you haven't thought this through."

"You're the one who isn't thinkin'," Clint retorted. "There are animal and vehicle tracks all over the place. Not to mention all the enemies you have. It'll take forever to sort through them all. But more importantly, no-one will be sorry you're gone. Just the opposite. Elk Valley will probably hold a parade to celebrate. But enough. Where's my stuff, or do you want the last ride of your life to be in this ATV sailing over a cliff, right here, right now?"

CHAPTER TWENTY-NINE

The question hung in the air.

Studying Dirk's expression in the fading light, Clint sensed the burly biker might call his bluff. Then, like a gift from the heavens, Tiffany unexpectedly spoke.

"It's getting dark. I vote we tie him to a tree and leave him here overnight. Perhaps God will whisper in his ear, or even decide his fate. If he hasn't been chewed to pieces and he's still alive when we get back in the morning, we'll give him a chance to make things right. If he doesn't, we can take it from there, and if we send him off the cliff at least we'll be able to see it."

"Lettin' God decide, I like that," Matt remarked. "That has my vote. What about you, Clint? You're the one he's screwed over."

Clint had been watching Dirk closely.

The moment Tiffany had said *tie him to a tree and leave him here overnight,* Clint was sure he'd seen a flash of terror in the burly biker's eyes.

"Sounds good to me. A night alone in a dark forest might be just what he needs to realize a few things."

"It's not like he'll be alone," Devlin continued, lowering his voice. "He'll have the forest creatures to keep him company, and there are so many of them out here, little and big."

"No, no wait!" Dirk suddenly yelled, his voice an almost high-pitched wail. "Willoughby, the ghost town, everything's stored in the rooms above the saloon. It's there, I swear it. I'll take you myself."

"You won't be takin' me anywhere," Clint growled, "but we'll check it out. How many of your gang are there?"

"Two, but if there's a delivery there are more. Mostly just two though."

"Armed I assume?"

"Yeah, armed."

"Tiffany, he attacked you. This is your call," Clint said solemnly. "Do we leave him here?"

"He's earned a reprieve, but we have to keep him under wraps until we can check it out."

"It's the truth, I swear, just get me outta here," Dirk pleaded, his tough facade dissolving in front of them.

"Sure looks to be a pretty night though," Devlin muttered, gazing up at the darkening sky.

As he finished speaking, an owl hooted, and an unexpected breeze whistled around them.

"Fuck, fuck, fuck," Dirk groaned. "I'll tell you everything, how we got in your stores, everything, just get me outta here."

"Okay, Dirk, but leave anything out, or tell a single lie, and you're back here tomorrow night," Clint warned. "You got that?"

"Yeah, yeah, I got it. I got it."

* * *

Life-threatening situations weren't new to Dirk. He'd had a gun held to his head, a knife at his throat, and fought in more bar brawls than he could count, but the thought of being left in the forest had filled him with a bone-celling fear.

Even as Devlin turned the ATV around and they started down the steep slope, Dirk's heart continued to race, and he was bathed in a cold sweat. He would have promised anything to escape a night of dark, unknown terrors. But as Clint's home came into view, the outside lights came on, illuminating the driveway and porch. Dirk's panic subsided, and he was filled with hatred for the three cowboys...and especially the girl.

"I'll untie your feet so you can walk," Devlin declared as they came to a stop and Tiffany and Clint climbed off.

"I have a storeroom in the back of the house," Clint began as Tiffany walked quickly to the house. "It has no window, so there's no way out except through the door, but you're still stayin' tied up. Seems to me—"

"Hey, Clint," Tiffany interjected, calling from the porch. "Can I talk to you for a minute."

Looking across at her, Dirk noticed she was standing next to the guy they called Matt. Of the three men, he looked to be the toughest. He'd jogged up the slope, and from what Dirk could see, he'd barely been breathing hard at the end. As Clint left to join them, Devlin began messing with the rope. Dirk knew he was a famous stunt rider and roper, and now he believed the hype. The lasso had fallen flawlessly from above his head and dropped around his body, then pulled tight around him, pinning his arms to his sides. It had almost seemed like a magic trick.

"Devlin! Bring him in," Clint ordered, raising his voice and gesturing him over.

Looking warily at the dog as he was led to the porch, Dirk noticed the tough guy had left.

"I'll take you to the storeroom," Clint said, glaring at him. "There's a bathroom you can use on the way."

As he walked through the front door, Dirk knew he had to bide his time. He'd been in worse scrapes, and had always found a way out. This situation would be no different, and they'd be sorry, all of them, especially the girl. But stepping into the living room, his deep thinking about escape and revenge was abruptly interrupted.

He wanted to steal everything he saw.

The paintings on the walls, the expensive western themed lamps, the cowhide rug on display above the fireplace, the bronze statuettes sitting proudly on hand-crafted wooden pedestals, and the smaller pieces on the bookshelf. The place was a goldmine.

"How am I supposed to do anything tied up like this?" he demanded, glaring at Clint. "Will you unzip me and pull out my dick?"

"You're a disgusting pig," Tiffany muttered. "I can't handle being around him for one more second. I'll be in the kitchen if anyone needs me."

As she marched away, Dirk wanted to make a coarse comment, but seeing Matt striding up to him, he held his tongue.

The muscled cowboy grabbed his arm.

It was like a vice.

"Devlin's the rope expert, he'll free your hands just enough, then we'll both wait for you outside the bathroom door. But try anything and I'll break your arm in three-seconds, and that's just for starters. You know I can do that, right?"

"Yeah, I know it," Dirk grunted, looking him in the eye.

"Good, let's go, and I've just checked. There's nothin' in there that can help you, so don't bother lookin'."

CHAPTER THIRTY

In spite of Matt's admonition, when Dirk stepped into the small powder room and the door was closed, he immediately set about trying to find something that might help him escape. Carefully sliding open the top drawer beneath the counter, though he found various items neatly laid out, there was nothing helpful. The second drawer netted the same result. But the third was a jumbled mess, as though someone had unpacked a box of supplies and forgotten to sort through them. His heart leaping with hope, he began rummaging through the mess.

"Hey, what's takin' so long?" Matt's gruff voice accompanied by a loud knock startled him, but undeterred, Dirk continued his search. "Are you alive in there?"

"Yeah, yeah," Dirk yelled back, then abruptly caught his breath. Beneath a pile of face cloths at the very back, he discovered a brand new, straight-edge razor.

While the ropes laced around his upper arms allowed for only limited movement, he managed to stuff the razor down the front of his jeans. After running the faucets for a moment, he slid the drawer closed, then flushed the toilet and opened the door.

"About time," Matt grunted, grabbing him by the arm and hustling him out.

Though he'd felt Matt's grip earlier, as the muscled cowboy marched him down the hall Dirk was again surprised by his strength.

"There's a sleepin' bag and a pillow, Clint's idea," Matt declared, shoving him into a small, windowless room. "Count yourself lucky. If it was up to me you'd be on the bare floor with no blankets."

As Matt slammed the door shut, Dirk grinned. His wrists had been left untied.

Looking around he saw a couple of chairs, a stack of bottled water, cartons of canned fruit and vegetables, and a small step ladder. There was a wall clock, but it had stopped.

Wasting no time, he settled into a chair, pulled out the razor, unscrewed the handle, and carefully lifted out the blade. But his arms still tied around his body afforded very little movement, and he had an extremely difficult time placing the sharp edge against the rope.

He was almost about to give up when an idea sprang to mind.

Placing the blade back into the razor, he found the handle gave him the extra length he needed. While he couldn't cut the cord, he could slowly shave it away.

It was a long, tedious task, but when he'd broken through one rope, he was able to take out the blade and easily slice through the second and third, then the coiled bondage fell loose. Quickly disentangling himself, he crept across the room and placed his ear at the door.

Silence.

He tried the door handle.

To his shock, it moved.

He peered through the crack.

Directly across the hall, Matt sat in a chair, his arms crossed and his head down.

Holding his breath, Dirk pushed open the door just enough to slide through and crept past the sleeping cowboy. Praying the dog wasn't around, he continued through the house, slipped silently outside, then raced to his 4Runner.

It wasn't the quietest vehicle he'd ever driven, and as he

started it up he was careful not to rev the engine. Amazed no lights came on in the house, he turned the vehicle around and glanced in his rearview mirror.

There was still no sign of life.

Barely able to control his dark fears of the surrounding forest, he drove as fast as he dared down the track. Even with his headlamps on full beam, it was tough navigating the path ahead, and every time he checked his mirrors, he expected to see the cowboys catching up.

But they never appeared.

* * *

In the Master Bedroom, Tiffany had stripped off while Clint had started the fire. As she'd climbed into bed, he'd removed his clothes, then stretching out beside her, he'd propped himself up on an elbow and smiled down at her.

"You are one smart lady," he said with a grin. "Actually, I remember thinking a little while ago that you were brave, brazen and beautiful. I was right."

"Really? When was that?"

"The first night you were here?"

"That feels like ages ago."

"It sure does, but a lot has happened, and a lot more is about to," he added, leaning down and nuzzling her neck.

"Clint, that drives me crazy…" she mumbled, then moaned softly as he took hold of her wrists and held them on either side of her head. "That does too."

"I know," he purred, kissing his way down to her shoulder. "Remember, no yellin' or cryin' out. We're not alone in this house tonight."

"I don't think I'll be able to stand it," she whimpered as he moved his lips over one of her nipples and hungrily drew it into his mouth.

"You'll have to," he whispered, raising his head, "even when I do this."

As he sharply nipped the cherry tip, she gasped, then bit her lower lip as she stifled a yelp.

"See, you can control your squeals when you need to."

"But it was really hard."

"I'll show you what's really hard," he growled. Releasing her wrists, he straightened up, straddled her waist, and took hold of his stiffened cock. "*This* is really hard. Do you want it?"

"You're such a tease."

"Oh, sweetheart, you ain't seen nothin' yet. Answer the question. Do you want it?"

"Of course," she mumbled, squirming beneath him.

"Then reach into that nightstand and get me a condom."

"But I can't reach it."

"Try."

An unfamiliar glint flickered in his eyes. For a moment she thought it was just the reflection of the flames, then an odd expression crossed his face sending a flurry of excitement rippling through her body.

"I, uh..."

"When I give an instruction, I expect it to be obeyed. Don't you know that? Are you just bein' coy, or are you testin' me—again?"

CHAPTER THIRTY-ONE

Clint could sense her excitement, and her need to feel his control.

"If I have to spank you, I will, but I can't use my hand, too much noise. I'll have to use a nasty little stick. Do I need to fetch it, Tiffany?"

Her brow immediately crinkled.

"A stick?" she repeated, breathing the word. "No, definitely not."

"No, *Sir,*" he corrected her. "That's how it's goin' to be in moments like this. Are we clear?"

"Yes, and thank you," she whispered, gazing up at him. "Thank you so much…Sir."

The epiphany washed over him.

She'd been waiting for a man like him, just as he'd been waiting for a smart, sassy, submissive like her, and she'd needed reassurance that he was, indeed, that man. As a surge of emotion moved through him, he lowered himself down and rested his weight on top of her.

"It's okay, baby," he crooned, then pressed his lips on hers, gliding softly, then slowly increased the pressure until he was devouring her mouth with fervent passion. Finally breaking back, he fisted her hair, tugged it to the side, and leaned down to kiss her neck. As he sucked in her skin like a starving vampire, he found himself spurred on by her soft but ardent cries. Quickly reaching across to the nightstand drawer, he fished out a condom.

"Roll over and get on all fours," he ordered as he kneeled up and sheathed himself.

Gazing down at her curvaceous backside washed in the fire's amber glow, he longed to spank her until her skin shone like the embers. But worried about the noise he began pinching her skin, eliciting sharp gasps.

"If you have to cry out, make sure your head's in the pillow," he said sternly as he placed himself at her entrance, then grabbing her hips, he thrust forward.

Pumping slowly, he relished the feel of her warmth, then quickened his pace, but only for a few minutes before he had a sudden need to see her face. As he pulled out and flipped her onto her back, she stared up at him and raised her arms. Sliding back inside her, he lowered his body wrapped her into his arms.

"Are you okay, babe?"

"I just needed to be held like this," she whispered. "I don't know why."

"It's been a crazy couple of days, but you're safe now. It's almost over."

"Thanks to you."

"You too," he said firmly, beginning to thrust with slow, powerful strokes.

"That feels amazing. You're so strong."

She wanted to feel his power.

Pinning her arms at her sides, he quickened his pace.

When she let out a cry, he swiftly covered her mouth with his, kissing her fervently.

As she began writhing beneath him, he responded, vigorously pumping and thrusting his tongue between her teeth to stifle her loud moans.

Then he suddenly paused, and staying buried inside her, he moved his lips to her ear.

"You're gettin' close. Remember, you can't make any noise."

"I won't be able to stay quiet," she gasped, "I won't, I know it."

Slowly pulling out, he rolled her on her side, plunged into her depths from behind, and placed his palm over her mouth.

"I'm goin' to fuck you hard 'til you come. My hand will muffle whatever sounds you make. Understand?"

She nodded, then mewled softly.

Wrapping his other arm around her waist, he began to stroke, and as he felt her responding, he moved his arm from her middle to her breasts, roughly kneading and pinching her nipples. With her muted whimpers telling him she was drawing close, he increased his pace. Her muffled moans became urgent, and he unexpectedly felt a rush of energy surge through his loins. Squeezing his eyes shut, and determined to hold himself at bay until she'd exploded, he was about to slow his fervent pumping when she abruptly arched her back and tensed.

"Give it to me," he whispered, "give it to me now!"

As her climax seized her, he couldn't hold back, and his orgasm shuddered through his body, tumbling through him like a cascading waterfall. Burying his head into her shoulder and holding her in his powerful arms, he managed to choke back his groans until the last spasms waned, leaving him breathless and his heart pounding in his chest.

* * *

Though Clint was exhausted from the drama-filled day, and his energy had been sapped by his powerful climax, he couldn't rest. As Tiffany lay sleeping in his arms, he stared at the ceiling, running through the various scenarios that could play out in the coming hours, perhaps even days. Finally telling himself he had the upper hand, and he'd make sure Dirk Griswald was put out of business once and for all, he closed his eyes and finally drifted off.

* * *

* * *

Miles away, Dirk sped down a deserted highway, then nearly missing the turn-off, he swerved violently into a dirt road kicking up dust and small rocks. As the 4Runner fish-tailed, Dirk wrestled with the wheel. Finally managing to regain control, he pushed his foot on the accelerator and sped towards Willoughby.

He had a huge task in front of him.

Clearing out all the stolen goods he'd so effectively hidden for over a year. But there was a whole lot more than the proceeds of his late night thievery…

CHAPTER THIRTY-TWO

The following afternoon, Gwen was hand-walking Oreo around her property when she heard approaching vehicles. Tiffany had called earlier asking if she could board Molly and two other horses for a short time. Assuming she had arrived, Gwen returned the gelding to his corral, then walked quickly out to the courtyard. Two trucks rolled to a stop, but only one was hauling a trailer.

"Hello, Tiffany. I thought you were bringing Molly and another horse," she declared as Tiffany and Clint climbed out.

"Clint had a ranch hand drive up to his cabin so we didn't need to bring them down, but Devlin's brought Merlin back. Sorry, I should have called to let you know. So much has happened my head's been all over the place."

"It doesn't matter. I've had such a busy day I haven't had a chance to fill the stalls with shavings anyway."

"I'll take care of the shavings for you," Matt declared as he and Devlin stepped up.

"Gwen, this is Matt Thompson," Tiffany said. "Matt, this is Gwen, the owner of this awesome little barn."

"Nice to meet you, Matt. I've heard a lot about you. Didn't you just have a baby?"

"I sure did. He and his mother are visitin' the grandparents."

"How lovely, and hello, Devlin, how are you?" Gwen asked, smiling up at him.

"Hi, Gwen, great. How's Oreo?"

"Doing so well, and it's all thanks to you, but you must get your horse out of that trailer. Matt, follow me. The shavings are in a storage room just inside the barn."

As Matt, Gwen and Tiffany headed off, Devlin unloaded Merlin and led him to an empty corral, while Clint let Buck out of the truck and started playing with him. Once inside the barn, Matt began filling the stall with shavings, and Gwen and Tiffany moved in to the feed room, closing the door behind them.

"Okay, Tiffany, what's going on?" Gwen asked quietly.

"Can't you guess?"

"Please tell me you have information on Dirk Griswald."

"I sure do. It's a long story, but Gwen, we know where he's stashed his ill-gotten gains."

"That's great! We'll get Merlin into his stall and give him some hay, then we'll all go into the house. We can sit down with some coffee and you can give me all the details."

* * *

The sheriff had just finished reading the afternoon reports when his secretary knocked on the door and poked her head in.

"Yeah, Marilyn, what's up?"

"Deputy Garland just called in. He said he's spotted unusual activity in that ghost town, Willoughby. He doesn't want to investigate without checking with you. He counted eight men, and he thinks he also saw Dirk Griswald."

"Griswald? Damn," the sheriff muttered. "Did the deputy specify what kind of unusual activity?"

"He saw them carrying boxes and loading them into SUV's, but it's barren out there, and he's watching from quite a distance through binoculars."

"Tell him to stay outta sight but keep up the surveillance, and report any updates as they happen. Find out where the patrol boys are. Sounds like I'll need all hands on deck."

"Right away, Sheriff."

Rising to his feet, the sheriff walked across the room to the coffee machine. He always thought better with the rich beverage in his hand. Pouring the freshly brewed java into his favorite mug, he added fresh cream and sweetener, then lifted it to his lips.

Located in a flat, dry, deserted valley, Willoughby was too far afield to be a successful tourist attraction, though some had tried to turn it into one. Scorching heat in the summer, then bitter cold in winter, repelled even the most ardent history buffs. Blustery winds didn't help, and swirling dust devils were commonplace. It was an uninviting slice of yesteryear. A town that had promised gold, but delivered only frustration and broken dreams.

He grimaced, silently berating himself for not realizing it was the perfect place to hide stolen goods. But was Griswald moving his ill-gotten gains, or loading up to make a delivery?

"Sheriff!" Marilyn said urgently as she burst into the room. "It's Deputy Garland again. The SUV's in Willoughby are leaving. He said if he tries to follow he'll be spotted in a heartbeat. He's waiting for instructions."

"Dammit. Did he say how many?"

"There are three, and they're all taking off," she replied as the phone on her desk rang behind her. "Should I answer that in here? It might be him again."

"Yes, quickly."

"Hello, Sheriff's office," she exclaimed, snatching up the receiver. "Deputy Garland? Hold on, I'm with the sheriff and I'm putting you on speaker."

"Deputy Garland, good work," the sheriff declared. "What's goin' on?"

"Sheriff, there are three SUV's. Two are Fords, and there's a Toyota 4Runner. I'm pretty sure it was Dirk Griswald I saw climbing into the driver's seat. But the thing is, when they left they peeled off like fighter jets. The Fords headed off in opposite directions, and the 4Runner went straight ahead. It's just desert out there. I can't imagine where they're going."

"They'll be hittin' the main road at different points," the sheriff said hastily. "Start cruisin' and let me know the minute you spot one of them. Meanwhile, I'll set up some road blocks."

CHAPTER THIRTY-THREE

As Devlin, Matt, Clint and Tiffany sat at the kitchen table, Gwen served them mugs of coffee, then set down a couple of plates of cookies and joined them.

"Gwen, I had to tell these guys I'm working with the FBI and you're my field officer," Tiffany began. "Things were getting complicated. I couldn't keep it quiet."

"I figured as much, but fellas, for the record, I'm retired. This situation cropped up only because I found out Dirk Griswald is here. The agency's been after him for a while, and oddly enough, his cousin, Paul Darrow, happens to own a barn just down the road. Dirk's a slippery bastard, and his lawyer's even worse. Clint, I know he's suspected of robbing your stores, and you're all here because you had him under wraps and he got away. Do you know where he is now?"

"Thanks to Tiffany, we know exactly where he is," Matt said with a grin, and lifting his phone from his pocket, he placed it on the table. "See that red light?"

"You're tracking him?" Gwen exclaimed. "How did you manage that?"

"He showed up at my home in the mountains because he had a tracker on my truck," Clint interjected. "When we got him talkin', he said he's been storin' my merchandise in Willoughby. We were goin' to lock him up and call the sheriff, but Tiffany came up with a better idea."

"Of course she did," Gwen remarked, smiling at her protégé. "She's good at those."

"I have my moments," Tiffany quipped with a grin.

"So, what was it?" Gwen pressed.

"She suggested we take the tracker he put on my truck to find me, and place it on his SUV, then let him escape," Clint answered. "Matt knew how to connect it to his phone, and it worked. Dirk went straight to Willoughby, but now he's on the move again. He's probably gettin' everything outta there because he think's I'm about to show up."

"I do have one question," Gwen added, a frown suddenly crossing her brow. "Won't he know the tracker's on his car? Surely he's still getting it on his own phone."

"Uh, no," Matt replied. "I found his phone under the floor mat in his 4Runner. Not the best hiding place in the world. It's locked and I couldn't get in, but I have it in my truck."

"Great job, both of you," Gwen exclaimed, then picked up Matt's phone and stared at the screen. "This is odd. He's headed in this direction. Clint, he could be on his way back to your cabin. He's known to hold a grudge."

"I doubt it," Matt said skeptically. "He had a rough time with us."

"I bet he's goin' to Paul Darrow's barn," Devlin piped up. "Like you said, Gwen, it's just down the road from here, and it's empty."

"I didn't know that. What happened to his clients?"

"He only had four left, and after he was picked up by the sheriff they called and asked if they could move their horses over to my place. I said sure. I wasn't there, but Matilda's home right now cookin' up a storm for a big event she's caterin'. The point is, Paul's place will be empty."

Staring back down at the red dot on the screen, Gwen nodded her head.

"I think you're right," she mumbled. "I have to call this in, and I'd better get in touch with the sheriff as well. We need to work together. Excuse me."

* * *

* * *

The sheriff was busy arranging road blocks when his secretary stepped in and announced he had a call from the FBI Field office in Dayville.

"The FBI?" he repeated, staring up at her.

"Yes, Sheriff. The caller said his name is Agent McCaffrey."

Not sure what to expect, but thinking it probably had something to do with Dirk Griswald, he picked up the phone.

"This is Sheriff Hooper."

"Sheriff, Agent McCaffrey here. I'm calling in regards to a wanted man operating in your area named Dirk Griswald."

"Yes, he's involved with some serious crime here and I'm currently setting up roadblocks. He was seen leaving what we think was his base in a place called Willoughby. It's a ghost town. There are three SUV's. He's apparently driving a Toyota 4Runner, the other two are Fords, but they're all headed in separate directions."

"Please don't pursue them or stop them," the agent said solemnly. "We believe we know where he's headed, and this may be an opportunity to catch him with his gang and his hoard."

"You know where he's going?" the sheriff repeated. "How?"

"The how is irrelevant, but I have a problem. We're on our way, but it will be a while before we get there."

"Can I be of assistance?"

"Thank you, Sheriff, you certainly can. This is what I need you to do."

Though the sheriff listened quietly as the agent issued his instructions, more than once he wanted to interject with a suggestion, but thought better of it.

"If you need to reach me in an emergency you can call or text me," the agent continued. "Write down this number. One,

one, zero, zero, seven."

The sheriff scribbled it on his note pad and repeated it back, smiling at the reference to 007.

"We'll be seeing you shortly, Sheriff. Thanks for your cooperation."

"Goodbye, Agent McCaffrey," he replied, but the agent had already ended the call.

* * *

Dirk had sped across the dry, flat, valley floor, but when he reached the main road he stayed within the speed limit. While his men were transporting Clint's merchandise, along with a variety of other stolen goods, Dirk was carrying precious cargo worth a great deal more. He had to keep it safe for one more night. The deal would go down the following morning, and he'd walk away a wealthy man.

There were Happy Accidents, then there were gifts from the Devil himself.

News of his cousin's reckless interference at the horse show had spread like wildfire and he'd lost the last of his clients, then he'd been incarcerated.

Dirk couldn't have been more pleased.

He'd instructed his lawyer to make sure Paul stayed behind bars for the next few days.

Dirk had already planned to shift his stash from Willoughby to Paul's barn, but after spilling his guts to Clint and his cronies he needed to do it right away.

Finding the razor and escaping the cowboys' clutches had underscored Dirk's belief nothing could stop him.

He was invincible.

CHAPTER THIRTY-FOUR

Sheriff Hooper had to move fast.

Agent McCaffrey had asked him to surround Paul Darrow's barn and keep watch, but not allow Dirk and his men to detect even the hint of surveillance. But at least Dirk was being tracked.

"I'll give you a head's up when he's five minutes away," the agent had promised. "You've got about thirty-minutes to get your men in place."

Running out to his car, the sheriff climbed behind the wheel and began contacting his deputies as he raced to the scene. At least he knew the barn and the surrounding area. There was a small paddock at the back of the property, above which sat a gentle slope. Like most of the terrain in the area it was heavily wooded. The trees would provide plenty of cover.

* * *

Slowing down as he approached the small township, Dirk was beginning to feel uncomfortable about leaving his valuable goods at Paul's barn with everything else. At Willoughby, he'd kept it hidden away in what had once been a general store.

He was also concerned about the 4Runner.

The sheriff would probably know about it by now, and the cowboys would recognize it on sight. They'd even taken his phone from under the car mat. Fortunately, amongst the pile of stolen items, he had a stash of burner phones.

He trusted his instincts.

They never failed him.

It was time to swap the 4Runner for another vehicle.

Rolling to a stop at the side of the road, he placed a call to arrange the switch. His raspy-voiced contact said a black Audi SUV would be waiting in fifteen minutes.

Dirk's mind began to race.

Fifteen minutes was enough time to unload this cargo, but where?

It suddenly hit him.

He knew the perfect place to store the precious crates safely overnight.

"I need the vehicle delivered," he declared. "Here's the address."

"I'll be there in twenty, but that's an extra hundred."

"Yeah, yeah, whatever," Dirk grunted, then quickly ended the call and continued down Main Street.

Turning at the end of the block and entering a modest residential neighborhood, he was soon rolling to a stop outside Tiffany's home. He had stop there and drop off a gift anyway, and it was the last place anyone would expect to find him. She was miles away on the side of the mountain with a bunch of dirtbag cowboys.

Breaking into the house on his first visit had been a piece of cake. He'd simply poked around the small front yard until he'd found the spare key. They were usually beneath garden gnomes or planters. In Tiffany's case, it had been under a ceramic red and white-dotted mushroom. After he'd unlocked the door, he'd quickly put the key back in its hiding place in case he ever needed to return.

Grinning as he let himself in, he walked through the kitchen and into the garage. As he expected, it was empty. After raising the door, he hurried out to the 4Runner, backed it up and unloaded the first two heavy wooden boxes, but as he turned to reach for the third, his back twinged.

"Fuck!" he growled under his breath.

When the old injury would suddenly flare up it could last for days, and oftentimes, was extremely painful.

He stared at the last crate.

It was the widest and heaviest of the three, but the contents were unbreakable. He could drag it to the edge and let it fall to the ground, or take off the top and unload enough to make it light enough to lift it out. Deciding on the latter, he found a crowbar in the 4Runner and pried off the lid.

He had just finished moving the half-empty crate when he saw the Audi stop at the curb. Not wanting the driver to see his stash, he hurriedly placed the lid on the box, and threw his jacket over the unpacked items on the garage floor.

* * *

Clint, Tiffany and Matt were watching Devlin work with Oreo when Gwen rushed up with startling news. Dirk had veered off the main road, driven through town and stopped at Tiffany's house.

"He was there for a good twenty-minutes," Gwen declared. "I didn't want to tell you until he left."

"I don't understand. Why not?" Tiffany asked urgently.

"Because you'd want to go over there. He'll be here soon enough and in custody, then we'll have some answers."

"Look, he's turned down another road," Matt interjected, looking over Gwen's shoulder at the screen. "I know that area. It's mostly body shops and a couple of used car dealers."

"He'll be swapping vehicles," Gwen remarked knowingly. "That will be the end of our tracking, but we have to assume he'll still show up at Paul's barn. Excuse me, I need to alert everyone."

As Gwen hurried away, Tiffany marched away, crossed her

arms and stared at the ground.

"Hey, what's up?" Clint asked, walking up behind her.

"I want to go to my house," she abruptly exclaimed, spinning around to face him. "He wasn't there looking for me. As far as he knows, I'm still with you up at the cabin. He has no idea we came down here."

"How can you be so sure?"

"We've been tracking him, remember? No, he was at my place for some other reason other than me, and I want to know what it is. Besides, I need to pick up a few things."

"But, Tiffany, he could go back there."

"Excuse me," Matt declared as he approached. "The 4Runner is going further into that area towards the junkyard. I'm sure Gwen was right. Dirk swapped cars. Someone else is driving it now."

"And Dirk is probably on his way to Paul's property," Tiffany added, placing her hands on her hips.

"Hold on, Gwen's texting me," Matt muttered. "The sheriff just reported two white SUV's have been seen heading this way."

"See!" Tiffany exclaimed. "Dirk won't be far behind. Please, Clint, take me to my house."

"It's a bad idea," he said, shaking his head, "and don't you want to be nearby when the feathers start to fly?"

"I want to go back to my house," she replied stridently. "If you don't want to take me, fine, my car's here. I'll go by myself."

"Matt, would you excuse us?" Clint said calmly. "Tiffany and I need a private word."

CHAPTER THIRTY-FIVE

As Matt walked away, Tiffany braced herself. She fully expected Clint to scold her, or threaten to spank her for being so rude. But he just stared down at her.

"Aren't you going to say something?" she demanded, then hating the way she'd sounded, she hastily apologized. "Sorry, that came out wrong, and I didn't mean to be so, uh, brusque, when I said I wanted to go to my house."

"It's okay," he replied, lowering his voice and moving closer. "We're all under pressure."

"So, uh, you're not angry with me?"

"A bit, but I get it. Like I said, we're all under pressure. There's an old saying, it's not what life throws at us that counts, it's how we handle it. Next time you're feelin' panicky think about that. Now let's talk about this. Tell me more about why you want to go back to your place."

"First, I want to see if Dirk took anything. You may not have noticed, but I have some lovely pieces there. A few would be expensive to replace, and there are a couple of items that mean a lot to me. If anything's missing, I can ask him when he's arrested, maybe even find them still in his car."

"Ah, yes, I understand. You said that was the first reason. What's the second?"

"What I said before, I need a few things, though I suppose they can wait."

"Can you tell me what things?"

A soft smile curled her lips.

"Some sexy lingerie for you," she whispered, stepping

forward and leaning against him. "It was supposed to be a surprise."

"Ah, I see, now it's my turn to apologize," he murmured, taking her into his arms, "but now I'll be lookin' forward to it. Come on, let's go. We need to hurry."

"Maybe you're right, maybe we shouldn't," she said hesitantly. "Dirk's bound to show up at Paul's barn soon, and those two SUV's will be arriving any minute."

"Then we'd better hit the road."

"Really?"

"Yep, come on," he said, grabbing her hand and marching towards the courtyard. "Buck, come on boy!"

"Are you two takin' off?" Matt asked as they hurried past him and the dog galloped up.

"Yep, Tiffany's worried Dirk might have stolen some valuable pieces when he was at her house."

"But you could miss all the fun, and the FBI might—"

"We'll be back pretty quick," Clint declared, cutting him off.

"Clint, I'd like to take my car," she said as he started to his truck. "Do you mind?"

"Nope, not at all, but I'm drivin'."

* * *

Watching Clint and Tiffany speed away, Matt shook his head. Something wasn't right. It wasn't like Clint to miss the action, and when Dirk and his men showed up and were apprehended, Clint should be there to identify his merchandise.

"You look worried," Gwen remarked, walking up to join him. "What's wrong?"

"Clint! He just left with Tiffany to see if Dirk stole anything from her house. It doesn't make any sense."

Gwen grinned.

"Matt, it makes all the sense in the world."

"What am I missing?"

"What would you do if Becky was about to be near a major showdown between the FBI and a violent criminal gang?"

"Oh, of course," he said with a sigh. "I'd want her on the opposite side of town."

"Exactly, and don't forget, Tiffany is officially FBI. Knowing her, she'd want to be involved in Dirk's takedown and arrest."

"So he's managed to get her out of here in the nick of time. Looks like Dirk did him a favor goin' to her house."

"He sure did, but I've been thinking about that. Why was he there? I can't imagine it was to steal anything. He could have done that any time. Why now?"

"Huh, that's a good point. Any ideas?"

"Hold on, it's Agent McCaffrey," she mumbled, lifting her phone to read a text. "Dammit, they've hit construction on the highway and he's still twenty-minutes away. He's putting me in charge of the operation until he gets here."

"I thought you were retired."

"One-second," she mumbled, tapping out a response. "I'm reminding him, not that it will make any difference."

"What did he say?"

"Agents never retire, they just take long breaks until they're needed."

"Why do I suddenly feel as if I'm in a movie," Matt said with a chuckle. "I suppose you know I'm former Special Forces."

"I certainly do, and I'm very pleased you're here. Excuse me, I need to speak with the sheriff. I know exactly how to handle this."

* * *

Slowing down as he approached Tiffany's house, Clint

noticed a black Audi parked at the curb.

"Any idea whose car that is," he asked, pressing the remote control clipped on the visor. But as the garage door rolled up, he slammed on the brakes. Dirk was standing in the middle of the empty space holding what looked like a machine gun.

"Clint..." Tiffany gasped. "Holy crap."

"Call the sheriff and stay calm," he muttered as Dirk moved towards them pointing the powerful weapon. "I'm gettin' out."

"No! Don't! He'll shoot you!" she yelled, trying to be heard over Buck's sudden barking.

"Buck, hush up," Clint said sharply. "Don't worry, Tiffany. He wouldn't dare, not in this quiet neighborhood. Make the call," he said firmly, then stepped from the car, opened the back door to let Buck out, and marched forward.

"Buck, stay with me," he ordered firmly.

Though the dog was growling and snarling, he stayed at Clint's side.

"Stop, stop right there!" Dirk yelled as they neared. "One more step and—"

"And what?" Clint replied, cutting him off and continuing towards him.

"Stop, or I swear to God I'll blow your fuckin' head off."

"I don't think so. That's not loaded, nor are any of the other guns around here," he declared, waving his arm at the various weapons lying on the ground. "Don't be an idiot. It's over. You're screwed."

"The hell I am," he shouted, lifting the weapon and charging towards him. "You, that mongrel and that bitch are fucking dead."

CHAPTER THIRTY-SIX

As Buck charged forward and sank his teeth into Dirk's leg, a loud shot pierced the air. Letting out a wild wail and dropping his weapon, Dirk fell to the ground, clutching his arm and frantically closing his fingers over a wound spouting blood while bellowing loudly and trying to kick Buck from his leg.

"Get him off, fuck, my arm. Stop him, stop him!"

"Buck, back off," Clint shouted.

As the dog finally released his writhing victim, Clint wrestled Dirk onto his stomach.

"Here," Tiffany exclaimed, abruptly appearing and handing Clint a pair of handcuffs,.

"What the hell?" he exclaimed, grabbing them and securing Dirk's wrists as the thug continued to groan loudly. "Where did you get a loaded gun?"

"In a hidden compartment under the driver's seat, along with the handcuffs," she quickly explained, lifting her phone from her pocket and placing a call. "Gwen? I have Dirk. He has a huge cache of weapons and apparently planned on leaving them in my garage. He's been shot, and Buck bit him pretty good. Nothing's life-threatening but we need an ambulance."

"I'll handle it. Good work!"

"Thanks, we'll stay here until it arrives. What's happening there?"

"McCaffrey was held up, but I have the deputies waiting inside the barn ready to pounce on Dirk's guys as soon as they get out of the SUV's...and they're approaching right now. I have to go."

"Don't worry about sending a deputy over here," Tiffany said hastily. "I'll arrest this bastard, then send him off to the hospital and secure the area. Good luck and we'll see you soon."

"That was impressive," Clint declared as she ended the call.

"Thanks, but hold that thought," she exclaimed, then turned and ran back to her car.

"Why the fuck did she have to shoot me? My arm is killing me. Take the cuffs off."

"Why did you threaten us with a machine gun?" Clint retorted angrily, "and take the cuffs off, not a chance in hell!"

"Who is that bitch?"

"Hey, don't call her that," Clint growled, fisting Dirk's hair and banging his head back down on the concrete.

"Okay, man, okay," Dirk protested. "But what's her deal? How did she learn to shoot like that?"

"Why do you care?"

"I don't, I just—"

"She's FBI asshole. You are royally screwed."

"FBI? You're fucking kidding me."

"No, he's not," Tiffany replied, walking up and showing her badge. "Dirk Griswald, you're under arrest. You have the right to remain silent. Anything you say can and will be used against you in a court of law. You have a right to an attorney. If you cannot afford an attorney, one will be appointed for you. Where did you get these guns?"

"I'm not saying shit without my attorney present."

"No problem, but trust me, not even your slimy lawyer can get you out of this mess. Excuse me. I hear a siren. Buck, come with me. You need to get back in the car."

* * *

The paramedics had been told Dirk was to be in an isolated

room with security personal until law enforcement officers could be assigned to guard him. As the ambulance sped away, Tiffany took photographs, and was about to lock the garage door and cordon off her driveway when a black Ford SUV with tinted windows suddenly came to a screeching halt in front of the house. Three men jumped out and marched across the lawn.

"Agent Tiffany Sullivan?"

"Yes."

"I'm Agent McCaffrey. Gwen gave me the run down. Brilliant job, brilliant."

"Thank you, Sir."

"And you are?" he asked, turning to Clint.

"My name's Clint Kincaid. I own a chain of western supply stores and Dirk Griswald has—"

"Yes, yes, I know. But it will take some time to have your merchandise returned."

"I figured as much. What about Dirk's gang?"

"They walked into an ambush. No shots were fired. Gwen is very good at her job. But you, Tiffany—may I call you Tiffany?"

"Yes, of course."

"You, Tiffany, have a bright future with the Bureau."

"Uh, thank you, Sir."

"Can we go back to Paul Darrow's place now?" Clint asked. "I'd like to talk to Gwen."

"So would I," Tiffany chimed in, "though I have to pick up some things here before we leave."

"You can go. I'll take care of this scene," McCaffrey declared, looking around the garage. "That's quite a stockpile of weaponry he had. It will be interesting to hear how he acquired it all."

"You might want to drive out to Willoughby," Clint suggested. "It's a ghost town, but he used it to store all this and everything else he stole. I have a feelin' there's a goldmine of forensic evidence out there."

"Gwen mentioned it. We'll be checking it out for sure. Tiffany, now we've captured Griswald your assignment is over. We'll close this house for the moment, so plan on packing up your things in the next few days."

"Ah, I see," Tiffany murmured.

"I'll be talking to the folks back at Langley about what comes next for you, but you've earned some serious brownie points. It won't be some ho-hum job in nowheresville. Goodbye for now. We'll be in touch soon. Oh, and go inside through the front door."

"Yes, of course, Sir."

As the agent turned away and began firing instructions to his men, Tiffany moved close to Clint and curled her fingers around his hand.

"Will you come inside while I pack?"

"Try and stop me," he softly replied, "but we'll talk about all this later. Right now I just want to get you over to Gwen's, then back up to the peace and quiet of my mountain home."

CHAPTER THIRTY-SEVEN

Wandering around the house with Buck while Tiffany packed her suitcase, Clint didn't notice any items that appeared particularly valuable, and assumed they were in her bedroom. When he poked his head in to check on her progress, he saw a few ornaments on the dresser.

"Okay, I think that's everything," she declared, zipping up her large suitcase. "I just have to throw away any perishables in the kitchen."

"What about those porcelain pieces?" he asked, nodding towards them.

"Those? They're not mine. Just part of the decor."

"Where are the items you said you were worried about?" But before he'd even finished asking the question, a bright red blush crossed her face. "Tiffany…?"

"Sorry," she mumbled. "I really wanted to come back here and you were so resistant, at least, you were at first," she added hastily. "I had to say something."

"Actually, I was looking for a reason to get you away from Gwen's."

"You were? Why?"

"I didn't want you there in case things got crazy. You know, like bullets flyin' through the air. But back to the point. If you didn't need to come back to see if Dirk had taken anything, why did you?"

"Do we have to talk about this now? Can't I tell you while we're on the way back to your place?"

"Yep, I want to get home too," he exclaimed, picking up her

suitcase. “Come on, Buck, out to the car.”

“Please don’t be angry.”

“I’ll reserve judgement until I hear why you felt you had to lie to me.”

“I still need to empty the fridge. It will only take me a minute,” she declared as they moved into the living room. “I’ll meet you there.”

As he turned and looked at her, he thought she seemed contrite, but it was confusing. They’d been through so much together, yet she’d held back her reasons for wanting to return to the house.

He suddenly wondered what else she’d lied about.

Not trusting himself to speak, he wordlessly strode to the front door and marched outside.

* * *

Tiffany pulled a trash bag from under the sink to empty the refrigerator, but there wasn’t much to clear out and it only took a few minutes. Walking out the kitchen door into the backyard, she moved swiftly to the garbage can. But lifting the lid, she caught her breath. Quickly closing it back down and dropping the trash bag on the ground, with shaking fingers she called Clint.

“What’s up, Tiffany? Do you need—?”

“You have to come into the yard—like—right now,” she exclaimed, cutting him off.

“I’m on my way.”

Slipping her phone back in her pocket, she tried to settle her nerves, but when the back door opened and she looked across at him, she knew there was panic in her eyes.

“Tiffany, what’s wrong?” he asked, striding towards her with Buck at his side.

“Prepare yourself. In the garbage can. Body parts.”

His dog was already sniffing around it, and suddenly began to bark.

"It's okay, Buck, quiet now," he ordered firmly, then slowly lifted the lid. "Damn, but, uh, Tiffany, they're not real, and what you think is blood looks more like ketchup. Probably is. Buck loves ketchup."

"Are you sure?"

"Positive. They're probably Halloween decorations. You wanna take another look?"

"Uh, not really, but I will," she muttered, steeling herself as she stepped up to join him. Staring down past the frighteningly life-like severed arm and foot, she realized he was right, then spotted a folded piece of paper. "Clint, I think there's a note."

"Damn, you're right," he said, peering back inside.

Quickly looking around, he found a stick and managed to flip open the paper without having to take it out. Written with a black felt-tip pen, it read, STAY OUT OF MY BUSINESS OR THIS WILL HAPPEN TO YOU.

"Obviously this is Griswald's doin'," Clint declared, "I'm callin' the sheriff and you need to call Gwen, but you can do that on our way home, and we're goin' right now."

"But I can't leave now, not with this in my backyard."

"That's precisely why we're goin'. This could be a set up to keep you here. We're reachable by phone, and if anyone wants to talk to you in person they're welcome to come up to my place."

"But—"

"This isn't up for debate. Dirk may be in custody, but he'll have friends," Clint said vehemently.

"I suppose you're right."

"Good, that's settled," he said, grabbing his phone from his pocket and placing a call. "Sheriff, it's Clint. I've put you on speaker so Tiffany can hear this. She just found what looks like human remains and a threatening note in her garbage can in the backyard. The remains aren't real, but I'm takin' her back up the mountain and we're headin' off now."

"Clint, I understand your concerns, but—"

"Sheriff, Dirk's behind this, and I'm not playin' his game. You can reach me any time, but we're outta here."

"I'm comin' over right now. Is Tiffany callin' Agent McCaffrey?"

"Not until we're on our way," Clint replied "I don't want him stoppin' her."

"Okay, Clint, but for the record, I'm obliged to ask you to stay."

"Not happenin'."

"Yeah, I got that. I'll be in touch."

As Clint ended the call, Tiffany threw her arms around his neck.

"Thank you, and I'm sorry," she exclaimed, hugging him tightly. "I'm an idiot sometimes. The thing is…I…uh…I sort of knew something like this was going to happen."

"Dammit, girl. Once we're on our way you'll tell me everything."

CHAPTER THIRTY-EIGHT

There was no conversation as Clint headed off to Gwen's. But the heavy silence was broken as two squad cars with their sirens blasting passed them, presumably on their way to the house.

"I feel weird not being there when they arrive," Tiffany muttered. "The sheriff might have questions."

"None that can't be answered on the phone," Clint replied. "Will Gwen be okay with you leavin' your car at her barn again?"

"Uh, yes, it's not exactly my car."

"Ah, of course, I should've realized. But your name is Tiffany Sullivan, right?"

"Clint!"

"Sorry, that was over the line, but—"

"But I can't blame you," she interjected with a sigh. "My middle name is Jane."

"Tiffany Jane Sullivan. That's pretty...like you," he added, lowering his voice and glancing across at her. "Yeah, I'm mad at you, but only cos I care about you so damn much."

"I care about you too," she said softly.

"I'll put your bag in the Jeep, then tell Devlin and Matt we're leavin' and what we found in that garbage can."

"They may have heard. The sheriff will have told Agent McCaffrey and Gwen, and Gwen may have told them."

"Regardless, they need to know we're takin' off. Don't take too long talkin' to Gwen. I wanna get movin'."

"I won't," she promised as he rolled into the barn and

stopped the car. "At least I don't have to find her. Here she comes."

Looking across the courtyard as he climbed out, Clint saw Gwen jogging up to them.

"Are you two okay?" she asked breathlessly. "I just heard about the gruesome stuff you found. I wonder how long it's been there."

"Who knows," Tiffany replied. "I'm just glad I didn't see it before today. I eat out so much I have very little trash. But, Gwen, do you have a minute? I need to talk to you."

"Sure, what's up?"

"I'll leave you to it," Clint said. "I'm off to find Devlin and Matt."

"They're with Oreo," Gwen remarked, "and your timing is perfect. Devlin's about to go home. You'll just catch him."

"Thanks, Gwen."

Striding across the courtyard and entering the barn, he found his buddies outside Oreo's stall watching him play with a hanging toy.

"Hey, I was just about to call you," Devlin declared. "Is it okay if I pick up Merlin tomorrow? I need to stay home tonight or Matilda will have my head. You may not know this, but Aussie girls can be tough."

"I think all girls can be tough," Matt piped up. "I swear, Becky's become a Mama Bear since Ernie came into the world."

"After what I just saw Tiffany do, I think I have you both beat," Clint said with a chuckle, "I still can't believe it, but sure, Devlin, no problem. Merlin can stay as long as you need. I just came in to let you know we're takin' off."

"Before you go, there are half-a-dozen boxes marked Kincaid in the storage shed," Matt continued. "The sheriff persuaded that FBI guy to bring them over and open them so you can check them."

"He did? Damn. I'll go out there right now. Thanks."

Hurrying back outside and across to the shed, Clint saw the large cartons placed side by side with the lids open. Moving from one to the next, he saw his valuable stock.

"I'll make sure you get that back as soon as possible," Gwen promised, walking in. "The wheels can move slowly, but I know how to oil them."

"I appreciate that, Gwen. Thank you."

"It's the least I can do. Your help with Oreo and connecting me with Devlin—it's been nothing short of miraclous."

"Horses are easy once you know how to speak their language. Will you be stayin' here now Griswald has been caught?"

"Heck, yeah. I'm retired! I'm not going anywhere."

"Then I'm sure we'll be seein' plenty of each other. Where's Tiffany?"

"She's on the phone talking to Agent McCaffrey, but I'll let her tell you about that," Gwen replied, glancing out the door. "Though it looks like she's finished. Now she's playing with Buck."

"Sounds like it's time to hit the road."

"Please drive safely."

"I always do."

* * *

Seeing Clint leave the storage shed and march towards her, Tiffany quickly opened the back door of the Jeep for Buck, then climbed into the passenger seat.

"I didn't want to keep you waiting," she said as he settled behind the wheel.

"Thanks. I just saw all the stock Griswald stole," he declared, starting up the engine and driving up to the road. "Sure was decent of the sheriff to get it moved over here for me."

"Gwen told me about that. I have some news too. I spoke to Agent McCaffrey and told him I wanted out. Before you say anything, I did it because this case made me realize an unpredictable life isn't for me. I don't want you to feel any kind of responsibility."

A frown crossed his brow, but he didn't say anything.

"I mean that in a good way," she added quickly.

"Yeah, I get that, but tell me about earlier."

"Earlier? You mean, why I wanted to go to the house?"

"Why did you lie? What's the big mystery?"

"I, uh, I get feelings about things, and I had this feeling I needed to go back there. That's the only way I can explain it. Like always, I was right," she finished, staring at him and trying to read his reaction.

"Tiffany, that's your inner voice, and we all have it. The more you listen, the stronger it gets."

"Exactly!"

"Why did you think I wouldn't get that, or was it something else," he asked pointedly.

"I was worried you'd try to stop me," she admitted quietly.

"Uh-huh, and you insisted on takin' your car because you had your gun and handcuffs under the seat."

"Uh-huh."

"So, how do you suggest we deal with this?" he asked, turning off the road and starting up the trail.

"You could hug me and kiss me and tell me I'm forgiven."

"I'll do that, and you are forgiven. What else?"

"Shit."

"Tiffany, you know I need to—"

"Punish me," she whispered, interrupting him.

"Yeah, but we have to talk about that later. Seems we have company."

CHAPTER THIRTY-NINE

Clint had noticed the silver Hyundai Sonata behind him a few minutes after he'd left Gwen's. He'd thought nothing of it, but when he left the main road and turned up the dirt track, the vehicle had followed.

"Are you sure?" Tiffany asked urgently, turning in her seat and looking through the rear window. "Oh, my gosh, that car can't drive up this trail."

"Apparently the driver doesn't know that, or he's a determined sonofabitch," Clint grunted. "Get into the back seat and hold on to Buck. I don't want him flyin' on the floor."

"What are you going to do?" she asked, hastily climbing across the console.

"Deal with whoever it is head on. Literally! Let me know when you're belted in and ready."

Though continuously glancing in the rear view mirror, Clint kept his eye ahead for the right spot to perform the tricky maneuver. When he saw it, he slowed down.

"Okay, I'm set," Tiffany exclaimed.

"Perfect timing," he muttered, then abruptly pressed down the accelerator and sharply swung the wheel, spinning the car around to face the Sonata and came to a sharp stop. "Are you and Buck okay?" he asked, hastily lifting his rifle from its overhead gun rack.

"Fine. What should I do?"

"Stay down."

Opening his door and using it for cover, he peered around

and studied the small sedan now stationary. Through his scope Clint could clearly see the passenger seat was empty, and the driver had both hands on the wheel. Taking aim at the tree closest to the car, he squeezed the trigger. As bark sprayed over the vehicle, the driver's door suddenly opened, and a man began frantically waving his arms above his head.

"Stop, don't shoot! Don't shoot!"

The voice sounded surprisingly young, and for a moment Clint wondered if he'd made a mistake, but quickly decided the car's presence was too coincidental.

"Turn around and walk backwards towards me, and keep those hands in the air. No sudden moves," Clint yelled.

Waiting until the culprit was halfway between the Jeep and his car, Clint ordered him to lie on his stomach. As the man followed the instruction, Clint ducked his head back into the Jeep.

"Tiffany, your cell phone should work from here. If it doesn't, the sat phone's in the glove compartment. Call the sheriff, tell him exactly what's happened and where we are. I'll be right back."

"Please be careful."

"This guy is scared shitless, but yeah, I'll have my guard up."

Striding to the back of the Jeep and opening the tail gate, Clint picked up the rope he always carried with him and marched to the man lying face down in the dirt. But crouching beside him, Clint discovered the man was more of a boy.

"How old are you?"

"Seventeen."

"What the hell? Why were you followin' me up this hill in a car like that?"

"I was ordered to."

"Who do you work for? Who sent you after me?"

"Dirk Griswald."

"What's your name?"

"Ben. Ben Clarke."

"Ben, Dirk Griswald has been hauled away by the FBI, and so has his gang. Don't mess with me. Someone else must've given you the order. Who was it?"

"His lawyer, Joseph Arnold. I never talk to Dirk personally, only Mr. Arnold. I was supposed to follow you and report back for more instructions."

"The sheriff's on his way, and you'd better tell him everything you know. If I hear you clammed up, I'll find you and you'll be sorry. Got it?"

"Okay."

"Learn some manners. Say, yes, Sir."

"Yes, Sir."

"Take my advice. Find a job you enjoy, not just a way to earn a fast buck, or you'll end up spendin' half your life behind bars."

"Uh, what are you going to do?"

"Tyin' you up so you can't go anywhere. The sheriff will be here soon. You got any weapons in that car?"

"There's a revolver in the glove box, but you can't leave me here. There are animals."

"Do you know the Lord's Prayer?"

"Huh?"

"You heard me," Clint said sternly.

"Yeah, I guess so."

"Stay it over and over again, then pray for a way to turn your life around. God might take pity on your sorry ass."

"Please don't go? I'll tell you everything, I'll tell the sheriff everything."

"Dammit," Clint muttered, tying the young man's hands behind his back. "Stay right where you are. Move, and I'm outta here."

"So, uh, you're staying?"

"Only if you do as I say."

"I will, I swear."

Walking briskly back to the Jeep, Clint climbed in and slid his rifle back into its holder.

"Hey, Tiffany," he said with a sigh. "Did you reach the sheriff?"

"He's on his way, but what's happening? Who is that guy?"

"He's just a kid, and he's in way over his head. I guess Dirk's slime ball lawyer hasn't heard his client has been arrested. He ordered that boy to follow me. He's scared to death out here so I told him I'd wait until the sheriff arrived."

"You have to anyway."

"Ben doesn't know that, and I just hope he has enough information to get Joseph Arnold in a shitload of trouble."

"Ben?"

"That's his name. I wonder if he likes horses. He should work at a barn. That would help straighten him out."

"You old softie," she said with a grin, then leaving Buck in the back of the Jeep, she returned to the passenger seat, leaned across the console and wrapped her arms around his neck. "You really are a lovely man."

"You might not think so when we get home."

"What's that supposed to mean?" she asked, sitting back and staring at him.

"Don't play dumb with me. You know exactly what it means, and here comes the sheriff. Won't be long now, and this lovely man will have you at his mercy."

CHAPTER FORTY

The sheriff made quick work of finding the gun in the Sonata, then untied the young man, placed him in handcuffs, and sat him in the back seat of the squad car.

"Trouble just keeps findin' you," the sheriff remarked, marching up to Clint watching from beside his Jeep.

"Hopefully this is the last of it," Clint replied. "The last few days have been like a TV cop show."

"Huh, you're right. By the way, I've never seen that kid before. Any idea where he came from?"

"Not a clue. He said Joseph Arnold gave him the order to follow me, and that it supposedly came from Dirk Griswald. Given Dirk's in FBI custody I'm not sure how that happened. But I have a feelin' that boy will answer all your questions. With any luck, that slick lawyer may just find himself needin' representation himself."

"That would make me a very happy man," the sheriff declared. "I'll call if I need you, and I'm glad you and Tiffany are okay."

"Thanks. Don't count on seein' us for a while. We'll be hibernatin'."

"Wish I could," the sheriff remarked, then strode back to his squad car.

As the sheriff drove off, Clint climbed behind the wheel, turned the Jeep around and started up the trail.

"Okay, Tiffany. Back to business. You said you didn't tell me about goin' back to your place because you thought Griswald would be there and you didn't want me to stop you."

"That's right."

"For the record, I wouldn't have. Capturing that bastard was your job, and I wanted him under wraps just as much as you, maybe even more, but I would have made sure you had backup. After all your trainin', I can't imagine why you chose to go there without it. Can you explain why you didn't talk to the sheriff or Gwen?"

"I had nothing concrete to tell them. I couldn't just say, *I have a feeling.* And what if I'd convinced them to listen, and we'd shown up with a bunch of deputies and I was wrong? It would have been so humiliating. But I won't have to worry about a situation like that again, and I'm so relieved."

"Because you resigned?"

"Yes, it's like a huge weight off me. I didn't realize how wound I've been. It's like living on tenterhooks. I feel like I can breathe again."

"I'm glad, darlin'," he said, lowering his voice. "Sit back and enjoy the drive."

"I will," she said with a heavy sigh. "It's so beautiful up here."

* * *

In spite of the bumpy terrain, Tiffany loved every minute of the long drive up the mountain. But when Clint rolled to a stop outside his home, she couldn't wait to check on Molly. As they climbed from the Jeep, Jethro appeared from the house to talk to Clint. She said a brief hello, then hurried into the barn with Buck running along beside her. Both Molly and Leroy nickered for treats, which she happily provided, then she began cleaning the dirt off Molly. She was almost finished when she heard Jethro's truck start up and drive away.

It was just her and Clint.

Feeling butterflies suddenly flutter to life in her stomach, she put down the curry comb and headed into the house.

"There you are," Clint exclaimed, walking up to hug her.

"This feels so good," she murmured, closing her eyes and relishing the feel of his muscled arms around her.

"Sure does, darlin'."

He'd muttered the words, then his fingers slid into her hair and tugged back her head. As he pressed his lips against hers in a long, lingering kiss, she never wanted it to end.

But it did.

Abruptly.

"I have something to show you," he murmured, staring down at her intently.

"Should I be worried?"

"I'm not sure how to answer that, but no, I don't think so."

"You don't think so?" she repeated as he took her hand and led her down the hall.

"I wouldn't say you should be worried, not exactly, but prepare yourself for the unexpected," he said with a devilish grin curling his lips.

"Okay, now I am."

He chuckled.

"What? Worried or prepared?"

"You're a funny guy, Clint Kincaid."

"I thought I was a lovely guy," he retorted, opening the double doors to his bedroom. "Has that changed?"

"You're both! Lovely and funny."

"You know things always come in threes," he remarked, taking her into his walk-in closet. "Pretty soon I'll be lovely, funny, and something else."

"I can't imagine, and why are we in your closet?"

"One second, darlin'. You're about to find out."

Releasing her hand, he moved to what appeared to be built-in shelving against the back wall. As he touched the side, it swung around to reveal a secret opening.

"Oh, wow!" she exclaimed. "What's in there?"

"Come in with me and see for yourself."

With her butterflies wildly fluttering as they moved into the semi-darkness, she saw him touch a button on the wall. The space was suddenly filled with a soft glow, and she found herself surrounded by a stunning array of BDSM supplies.

"I don't know what to say," she gasped. "I'm…I'm…"

"Excited, I hope," he said, placing an arm around her shoulders. "This is who I am, but you already knew that—or at least suspected it—right?"

"Uh, yeah, but I never thought you'd bring me into a secret supply vault!" she exclaimed, trying to take it all in. "You have so much."

"You know I'm gonna spank your butt," he whispered, pulling her close to his body and lowering his lips to her ear. "It's time to pick your poison."

As he turned her around, she found herself looking at a wide variety of floggers, paddles, and crops.

"What's it to be you naughty girl? The choice is yours."

CHAPTER FORTY-ONE

The moment Tiffany had stepped into the decadent room, Clint had seen the excitement dance in her eyes, and he knew he'd found a kindred spirit. As he watched her try to make up her mind, he noticed her gaze wandering to the shackles.

"You can choose more than one, but if you take much longer I'll decide for you," he warned. "Now fetch what you want and bring it back to me."

She stared up at him, but only briefly, then stepped to the display and picked up a round, black leather paddle, and a short, fat riding crop with a wide tongue.

"Here you are, Sir," she murmured, handing them over.

"Have you been with a Dominant before?"

"Yes, Sir, in my fantasies," she said softly, tilting her head to the side.

"But you've read a lot."

"God, yes. I can't get enough of it," she replied earnestly, sending his cock stiffening to full attention.

"Now the restraints," he ordered, nodding to the area that had caught her eye.

He heard her catch her breath, and as she walked over to the wall, he thought she looked like a kid in a candy store.

"These," he declared, quickly striding up and choosing fur-lined nylon cuffs with velcro fasteners. "That's it for now," he continued, guiding her back into his closet. "Take off all your clothes, then stay in here and wait for me to come and get you. Any questions?"

"No, Sir."

* * *

* * *

Excited but nervous, Tiffany waited until Clint left and closed the door behind him, then turned back to stare at the entrance to the salacious supply room.

It was still invitingly open.

Hoping she'd be able to spend hours there learning about every toy, she peeled off her clothes and set them on one of the shelves. When Clint returned just a few minutes later, he was wearing a bathrobe, and wordlessly taking her hand he led her into the bedroom.

The blackout curtains were closed.

A fire blazed.

Fat candles burned.

The bedclothes were pulled down.

The cuffs, paddle and crop sat lined up at the end of the bed, along with condoms.

"Tiffany," he began softly, placing his hands on her shoulders, "there are two simple rules. Do as you're told, when you're told. If you don't, you'll be punished. If you think something is becoming too much, say orange. If it actually becomes too much, say red. Any questions?"

"No, Sir."

"Lift your wrists."

As she raised them, he swiftly cuffed her, then bent her over the bed. Her butterflies suddenly turned into tiny tornadoes, but they became the last thing on her mind as he began spanking her, swiftly traveling his flattened palm from cheek to cheek with hot slaps.

"Why am I doin' this?" he demanded sternly, increasing the force and speed.

"Because I wasn't straight with you. I'm sorry," she cried,

unable to stop herself from squirming.

"You didn't trust me enough to tell me what was goin' on," he exclaimed. "I know you think you're a one woman army, but you're not. Are we clear?"

"Yes, Sir! We're clear!"

"Climb on the bed, then get on all fours with your legs apart and your face on a pillow."

* * *

Stepping back and watching her take up the position, Clint slipped his hand under his robe and stroked his hardness. Her curvaceous ass was bright red, and he spied her pussy's glistening need. He longed to thrust inside her warmth, but she was expecting more, and he wasn't about to disappoint her.

Picking up the leather paddle, he kneeled behind her and thrust his finger into her slick sex. As she salaciously wriggled her hips, he swatted her right cheek, eliciting a loud squeal.

"Does it feel the way you imagined it would?"

"Uh, it hurts so much more than I thought."

"How many do you think you deserve?" he asked, swatting the left.

"Ow, oh, Sir."

"How many?" he repeated, smoothing the cold, hard leather over her crimson skin as he fingered her passage. "And Tiffany, think carefully before you answer."

He could hear her panting, and knew she was having a tough time trying to focus.

"Uh, it's not for me to say, Sir."

He grinned.

"You are one smart girl. You'll be rewarded for that," he muttered, rubbing her clit and loving her moans and wriggles. "But first you'll get a few more."

Moving to her side and wrapping his arm around her waist, he delivered the stinging swats slowly, ignoring her squeals and yelps, and making sure she felt the full impact of each blow.

"Are you sorry you chose the paddle?"

"No, Sir," she moaned as he finally dropped the wicked implement and rubbed her burning skin. "I wanted to experience it. But I won't ask for it again. At least, I don't think I will. My ass is on fire."

"And you're so wet," he grunted, teasing her pussy with his cock as he continued to smooth his palm over her scorched backside.

"Sir…I want you so much," she whimpered, arching her back.

As her urgent plea sent a fresh wave of energy through his loins, he snatched up a condom, ripped open the packet, and swiftly sheathed his rigid rod. But rather than plunge inside her slick depths, he continued to tease her, rubbing her clit and placing his hardness at her entrance, only to pull back.

"I promised to reward you," he purred, leaning over her body and whispering in her ear. "Close your eyes and stay exactly as you are. I'll be right back."

CHAPTER FORTY-TWO

Though Tiffany's skin was stinging, never had she felt so alive, or filled with such carnal hunger. But when Clint returned and climbed back on the bed, she held her breath, not sure what to expect.

Then she heard it.

The subtle hum of a vibrator.

As it pressed against her clit, she let out a wild cry, then he was suddenly inside her, thrusting in and out with slow, strong strokes.

"Do you like your reward?" he growled as he pumped.

"So much," she gasped. "Please don't stop."

"You're not allowed to come without permission. Is that clear?"

"Ooh, yes, Sir," she mewled, not sure if she could obey, but as the buzzing implement continued its delicious, dizzying dance, all thought left her. Waves of glorious pleasure rippled through her sex, and his member possessed her as it plunged in and out of her passage.

But he suddenly pulled out, and the crop's fat leather tongue began landing on the back of her thighs with quick, hot strikes. All the while the vibrator continued to send its scintillating sensations through her pussy. The combination of pleasure and pain became a whirlwind of tantalizing torture, and a powerful climax rising up inside her threatened to take hold.

"I'm going to come," she gasped. "I can't stop it."

The words had barely escaped her lips when the vibrator stopped, and the crop no longer nipped her skin.

"Just as well you told me," he said huskily, placing his member against her entrance and gripping her waist with his strong hands. "Your ass is red, but it would be a whole lot redder if you hadn't."

Though she heard him, she was out of breath and too dizzy with need to respond. But as he plunged back inside her, she let out a cry and bucked back.

"You need me to fuck you hard, don't you, darlin'?"

"Yes, yes," she muttered, loving his stiff rod slowly thrusting in and out of her.

"How much do you need it?"

She caught her breath.

"How much?" he repeated sternly, landing an unexpected slap on her singed backside.

"Ooh, please, Sir, please, I'm begging you, I need you to fuck me hard, or slow, or however you want, but please—will you fuck me until I come?"

As she'd stammered out her plea she'd meant every word.

She was loving his control, and being at his complete mercy.

* * *

Clint had enjoyed his experiences in the BDSM world. He was a member at a couple of high-end clubs, and he'd shared his bed with women who claimed to need what he offered. But he never quite believed them, or sensed the connection he longed for.

Tiffany was different.

She was real.

Every fiber of his being could feel her submissive longing, and it burned through his soul like a flame blazing down a match. His dominant control fueled her erotic fever, just as her surrender fed his dark, carnal desires.

"Please, Sir…?"

Her ardent, heartfelt request snapped him from his reverie. Leaning over her body and slipping his hand beneath her, he tweaked her nipples and roughly kneaded her full, luscious breasts, making her squeal and wriggle.

"It's time," he breathed, his lips pressed against her ear.

Hearing her gasp, he straightened up, clasped her hips and began to thrust. Though he started with slow, strong strokes, he gradually accelerated until he was pumping with gusto.

But a thought suddenly sprang to mind.

Abruptly stopping and pulling out, he rolled her onto her back, swiftly took off her cuffs, then stretched out beside her and deftly moved her on top of him. Hastily straddling him and holding his cock, she closed her eyes and lowered herself down.

"You're not going to move," he ordered, picking up the vibrator and placing it against her clit. "Just let it happen."

"You mean I can come when I feel it, Sir?" she whimpered. "Ooh, that feels so good."

"Yeah, that's what I mean," he grunted, watching her face crinkle as the divine sensations rippled through her pussy.

It was only moments later her soft moans grew louder, then became series of shrill cries. As the tingling buzz radiated through his member, and her pussy walls pulsed against him, there was no stopping the powerful climax rising up from deep inside him. As it jettisoned through his loins and exploded from his cock, he couldn't hold back his deep guttural groans…

* * *

Feeling wonderfully weak in Clint's strong arms, Tiffany couldn't remember ever feeling so happy.

She was in love.

Madly, deeply, crazy in love.

But was he?

"Clint…?"

"Yeah, darlin'?"

"What happens now?"

"We take a few days to recover from the madness we've just been through, though I guess bein' with the FBI you're used to all that."

"Lord, no," she muttered. "I've been on cases, but nothing like what just happened. I suppose I need to find something else now."

But the thought of leaving him and his mountain home sent a wave of sadness through her heart.

"There's no rush, and like I said we need some down time. Tomorrow I'll take you on a trail ride. The horses need to get out, and I know you'll love it."

"That sounds perfect."

"Are you hungry?"

"Starving," she replied, snuggling against him, "but I hate the thought of getting out of this bed."

"It'll still be here," he said with a chuckle, "and tonight we're goin' back into my supply closet. I wanna show you a few things, then we're comin' back here and I'll take my time explorin' every inch of your gorgeous body."

"That sounds amazing," she whispered, trying to swallow back the unexpected lump in her throat.

"Hey, what's wrong?" he asked softly, tightening his hold, "and don't say nothin'. I can feel it."

"You can?"

"I sure can, now tell me, and don't hold back."

"I care about you—a lot," she managed, "and at some point I'll have to leave."

"Hey, you're not goin' anywhere," he murmured, rolling over and gazing down at her. "Tiffany...don't you know I'm crazy about you?"

"You are?"

"Hell, yeah."

"But that closet...surely you must have had—"

"Stop! I'm no saint, but there's never been anyone like you," he said solemnly. "You're the real deal."

"What does that mean?"

"I guess I need to say it." he said with a sigh. "Tiffany Sullivan, you came into my life and hit me like a ton of bricks. Yeah, I love you..."

"Thank God," she whispered. "I love you too, and I was really scared there for a minute. I've never met anyone like you, or felt like this."

"Like me?"

"You're good, but in a very real way, you're bad too."

He grinned.

"I'll tell you what I told Dirk. There are good guys, there are bad guys, then there are cowboys, and that's what I am."

EPILOGUE

The following day Clint received a call from the sheriff with unexpected news about the young man who had been driving the Sonata.

"Ben Clarke's mother is Jessica Clarke, the same Jessica Clarke who works for Matilda Pike," the sheriff began.

"Matilda? Devlin's wife?"

"Yep. Turns out Ben was a stable hand for Paul Darrow, and when Paul lost most of his clients Ben had to go, but Paul had another job lined for him with Dirk Griswald."

"No!"

"Apparently Ben's father passed away a couple of years ago and it's been tough goin' for him and his mom."

"Poor guy."

"Clint, I've spent some time with him and he's a good kid. He volunteered everything he knew about Dirk's lawyer, Joseph Arnold, and that gun in the glove box only had Dirk's prints on it. Ben never touched it. He told me guns scare him. So, bottom line, I sent him over to Gwen's. She needs the help, and I think he deserves a second chance."

"It sure sounds like it, but why are you tellin' me all this?"

"You're the one he was followin' up the hill and had the problem with."

"Sheriff, I trust your judgement. If you think givin' him a break is best, it's fine with me."

"Good to hear, thanks, Clint. I also wanted you to know where he'll be workin' so you're not surprised if you run into him, which you probably will. But I'll be keepin' my eye on him, and if anyone can keep him on the straight and narrow, it's Gwen."

"He could end up workin' for the FBI."

"Damn," the sheriff muttered. "That would be one for the books!"

* * *

After several salacious nights, sleeping late, idyllic trail rides and romantic dinners on the terrace at sunset, it was time for Clint to turn his attention back to his business.

On the top of his agenda was finding a solution to the vulnerabilities exposed by the burglaries. He was on a conference call with a security company when Tiffany brought him a cup of coffee. Settling into a nearby chair, she quietly listened to the conversation.

"I don't know what to think," he exclaimed as the call ended. "Sometimes it was like they were talkin' a foreign language, and they kept throwin' all these different products at me. Isn't it up to them to make the best recommendations?"

"Are you asking for my opinion, or are you just blowing off steam?"

"Absolutely I want your opinion."

"Then without meaning to sound critical, some of the equipment they suggested is outdated," she remarked, rising to her feet and walking across to sit next to him.

"How do you know?"

"Security systems, alarms, how they work, the latest and the greatest, all that stuff, was part of my training. So was profiling."

"Profilin'?"

"Employees. You'd be surprised how much commercial and industrial theft involves inside help...and why are you looking at me like that?" she added as he leaned forward and grinned.

"Tiffany, I was already thinkin' about this, but you've just made it no-brainer Will you be my head of security and oversee all this?"

She took a startled breath, then smiled back at him.

"Well, Mr. Kincaid, that depends on the perks. What are you offering?"

"Let me put it this way," he replied, lowering his voice. "If you refuse, I'm gettin' that paddle."

"Ah, I see. In that case I'd love the job," she said hastily, "but it means visiting each of the stores. They'll have different needs."

"Yeah, I get that, and I have to see them myself after everything that's happened. We'll go together. Durin' the day, you'll be Head of Security doin' whatever it is you do, while I deal with a bunch of other stuff."

"And at night?" she murmured, slipping off her chair and into his lap.

"At night…you'll have to wait and see. Just bear in mind the stores offer a variety of innocent lookin' items that can be used to take a naughty girl in hand!"

* * *

A couple of weeks before the first winter storm, Clint and Tiffany moved to his house overlooking the lake. Though Clint usually boarded his horse with Devlin, or at Lone Pine Ranch with Callum, the facilities were full. But Gwen had room for both Molly and Leroy. When Clint and Tiffany rolled up, she had nothing but praise for Ben Clarke. The young man had been a Godsend.

In the middle of December, Clint decided to throw a holiday party. He invited Matt and Becky, Callum and Kelly, Devlin and Matilda, Gwen and Ben, and Ben's mother Jessica.

Tiffany threw herself into the project, and insisted on inviting the four-legged members of the group as well. Matt's dog, Shelby, Callum's amazingly smart Labrador, Waggles, and Cinders, the Doberman Devlin had adopted.

When she suggested the evening could be catered by The Barnyard, a popular local restaurant. Clint agreed, but he wanted to cook the Turkey himself. Though she was skeptical he proved up to the task, and standing proudly at the head of the table on the big day, he sliced the juicy meat, then raised his glass in a toast.

"We're friends, but I see you as my brothers and sisters. We're a family, Elk Valley is our home, and that amazin' tree on top of Lone Pine Hill stands guard over our little community. To us!" he declared.

As they raised their glasses and drank the champagne, Tiffany felt her heart swell. Everything was perfect.

Well…almost.

All the couples at the table were husband and wife.

Except for her and Clint.

* * *

When everyone had left, she was picking up the dishes when Clint walked up and brought her into his arms.

"Hey, thanks for all the effort," he said gratefully. "You did an amazin' job."

"And you cooked an amazing turkey. I wasn't sure about that."

"Yeah, I know," he said with a chuckle, but as a frown crossed his brow, her pulse ticked up.

"Clint, is something wrong?"

"No…not wrong…I'm just not sure where to start. Tiffany, you came into my life outta nowhere. I looked up, and there you were, standin' next to your horse in my dirt driveway lookin' lost and bedraggled. I swear, time stood still. This might sound crazy, but think I fell in love with you right then."

"Clint..."

Breaking their hug, he produced a black velvet box from his pocket. With her heart pounding, and praying her Christmas wish was about to come true, she took it from his hands and lifted the lid. A gold ring boasting a horse's head with diamond eyes, encased in a heart, stared up at her.

"Clint, it's the most gorgeous thing I've ever seen."

"Every time I look at you, I can't believe how lucky I am," he murmured, lifting it from the box. "It was Molly who brought you to my mountain home that day. She carried you up that long trail to my door. This ring is a tribute to her, as well my way of sayin' I love you, and I want you with me always. I can't imagine ever bein' with anyone else. I guess what I'm tryin' to say is, will you spend the rest of your life with me? Will you marry me, Tiffany?"

"Yes, yes, yes," she exclaimed as happy tears spilled from her eyes. "I can't s-speak. It's just s-so b-beautiful."

"I don't want you to speak," he said huskily, slipping the ring on her finger. "All I want you to do is kiss me."

THE END

Dear Reader:

Thank you for buying this book. If you have a moment I would greatly appreciate your review. I constantly strive to bring you interesting and enjoyable content and your feedback is valued. Feel free to contact me at any time. I love to hear from readers. My email is: MagCarpenter@yahoo.com, and here are my social media links should you care to check them out.

My very best wishes,
Maggie

http://www.MaggieCarpenter.com
https://www.facebook.com/MaggieCarpenterWriter
https://www.facebook.com/maggie.carpenter.792

To View My Other Novels
https://www.amazon.com/Maggie-Carpenter/e/B0034QAYIU/

Made in the USA
Columbia, SC
30 October 2024

45266438R00107